# FIGHT, FLIGHT, OR SHIFT

## BILLIE BLACKWATER, BOOK ONE

### KIRA BRINAMON

Published by Blue Unicorn, an imprint of World Weaver Press, LLC
Albuquerque, New Mexico

Cover layout and design by Sarena Ulibarri
Cover images used under license from DepositPhotos.com.

ISBN-13: 978-1-7340545-3-8

Also available as an ebook.

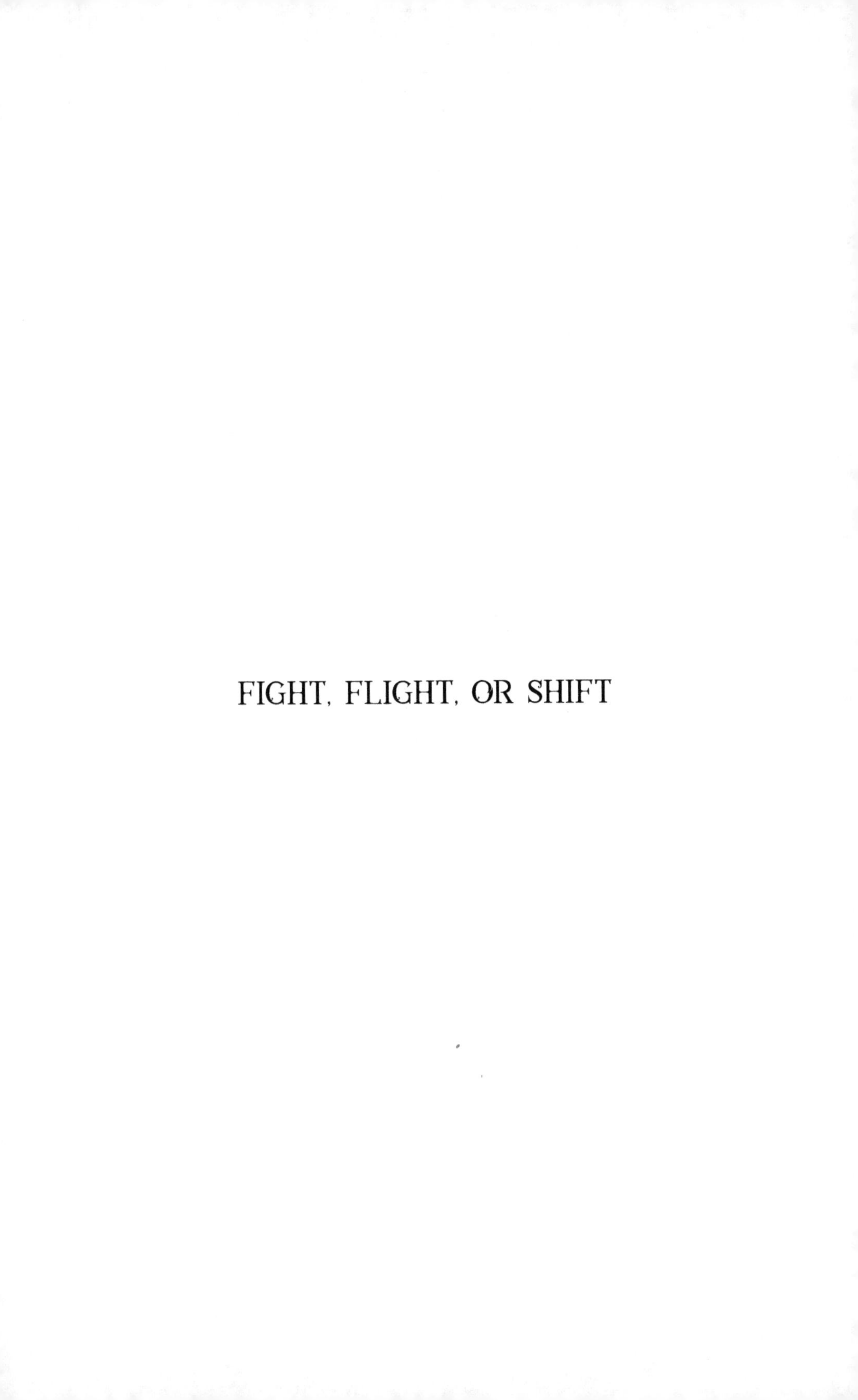

FIGHT, FLIGHT, OR SHIFT

# SUNDAY

Billie had gotten roped into leading the ghost tour at the Silver Coin Hotel, again. She certainly believed in *some* supernatural phenomenon—she knew quite personally that things were not always what they seemed—but the ghost tours were just another of Mitch's tourist traps, a way to transform the rather mundane history of the mountain town of Juniper into cash.

Today's tourist group included a mother and a shy ten-year-old boy, both adorned in way too much denim and wearing matching turquoise cowboy hats that Billie recognized from a shop on Miners Avenue, as well as a young couple in flip flops and shorts. Billie watched the four of them while she wiped down the bar top and mentally steeled herself to pretend to be a ghost expert. The boy hid behind his mother and peeked nervously at the taxidermied bear, and the couple sat in the chairs below the antler chandelier, scrolling on their smartphones. Out of excuses to delay, Billie sighed and went out to the Silver Coin's lobby.

"Good evening! My name's Billie Blackwater," she announced, "and I'm a lifelong resident of Juniper, one of the most haunted towns in Colorado." It wasn't, it *really* wasn't, but this was part of the script Mitch had told her she had to memorize. "If you'll follow me up this staircase, I'll be happy to share all of the Silver Coin Hotel's secrets with you."

In truth, she would be happy to let Juniper keep all of its secrets, whether supernatural or mundane, from the people who came up to hike in its forest or canoe on its lake, the tourists who were only there for a day and left trash on the trails and Jeep ruts in the dirt roads. The local mine had closed a generation ago, so town's economy depended on the tourists now, but that didn't stop Billie from resenting every unfamiliar face that entered her forest. And besides, she wasn't going to reveal *all* of the Silver Coin's secrets in this ghost tour; one whole floor of the hotel held Mitch's hidden casino, accessible only by a code that she was guessing no one in this group had been told. The casino was one reason Mitch insisted on maintaining the ghost tour: to explain away any odd sounds that might leak out of the secret room.

Billie stopped at the first landing and pointed toward a large arch-top window that overlooked the lake, telling the group how on certain nights, if the moonlight was *just* right, you might see a woman in white looking back at you through the glass. Everyone nodded somberly, snapped pictures of the window, and followed Billie up the flight of stairs to the next attraction. In front of a hotel room door labeled with the ominous number of 13, she told them about a guest whose belongings were unpacked and strewn about the room every time he left. At a storage closet, she described the maintenance man who had supposedly been found dead in there. Near the blocked off staircase to the upper floor, where the casino was, she told the story of Reno Bridges.

"In the year—" She couldn't remember the year it was supposed to be, so she picked one at random. "—nineteen-fourteen, Juniper was a booming mining town. The Silver Coin's top floor was a dancehall, where all the miners and their ladies came to dance and drink. It was owned by Reno Bridges back then, and he was a busy man, always worried about his business, always taking care of the patrons who frequented his establishment. Well, his wife got tired of being ignored, and of watching everyone else have fun while she had no one to dance with. So she started up an affair with one of the newest prospectors in town, dancing with him every night. And when Reno Bridges finally noticed what was going on and confronted his wife's lover, the man pulled a knife and stabbed him, right in the middle of the dance floor. He bled out there, with everyone watching. His wife took over the Silver Coin after that, with her new husband, but attendance at the dancehall began to drop because the miners shared strange stories. They said they still saw Reno Bridges. They'd go to get a drink and he'd be there at the bar, covered in blood and dripping all over their whisky glass. They said they'd see a man lurking near their wife, but when they approached, they could see right through his skin to his skeleton. Finally, the dancehall closed, and the stairway was blocked off. Sometimes, even now, we hear things that let us know that Reno Bridges is still up there, plotting his revenge."

As if on cue, a rattle and thump came from just overhead. The tourists all jumped. Billie tried not to roll her eyes. Some rancher had probably just bet away his favorite bull, again, or someone was going to have to wash someone else's truck for a year because they bluffed when they should have folded. It was mostly locals who played Mitch's games, and they traded as much in goods and favors as they did in money, since even the richest residents of Juniper didn't have a lot to throw around. Mitch strutted around like he owned the town and took his illicit activities *very* seriously, but to Billie the guys in the casino often seemed like little kids playing dress-up. Of course, she'd never tell Mitch that. And of course, since the tourists didn't even know the casino existed, what other explanation could there be for the thumps and creaks except a ghost?

She gestured toward the bird cage elevator next to the blocked-off staircase, and suggested the ghost tour group take the elevator back down to the first floor. The doors opened to let them out near the hotel bar where Billie usually worked, where she'd have to go back to as soon as she finished the ghost tour. But the tour was supposed to be an hour long, and she still had twenty minutes to fill. What was that one Kim had made up about the kids who had broken into the Silver Coin while it was abandoned? She started to tell it as she led them down the hallway, making up the details she couldn't remember.

"Excuse me," one of the tourists interrupted. Billie turned to see one half of the young couple, standing with a hand on her hip and lips pursed. Billie looked between the couple. They were probably around Billie's age—mid-twenties, anyway—and the man wore a Denver Broncos shirt, while the woman's graphic t-shirt featured some band Billie had never heard of. "That's not the same version we heard last time we were here," the woman in the band t-shirt said.

*Crap*, Billie thought. "Well if you had Kim last time, she does tend to embellish…"

The woman shook her head. "No, see, we're amateur ghost hunters, aren't we honey?" She looked to the man in the Bronco shirt, who nodded eagerly. "And this story is very well documented by a blogger that we follow. There's even a picture."

"Well," Billie faltered. "There have been lots of pictures of orbs taken in this hallway…"

"Not *orbs*," the woman said, exasperated.

Just then, the elevator doors down the hallway clanged open, and Billie looked past the tourists to see Mitch holding onto a man's shirt like a cat held by the scruff of the neck. It was Daniel Gadbury: a regular on the casino floor, one of those locals who sat up there gambling away their family's land or their earnings from the quarry. Daniel's face was beet red, and Mitch looked pissed. *Wonder what he did this time*, Billie thought as Mitch pushed him so he stumbled out into the hallway, hitting the wall and tumbling onto his side. Probably tried to cheat, or insulted one of Mitch's fancy out of town friends. The tourists stared aghast as Daniel groped at the wall, struggling to stand. He staggered toward the double doors that would let him out to the parking garage. Mitch made eye contact with Billie, then crooked his fingers in a quick "come here" gesture.

"Sorry, excuse me for just a minute," she told the tour group. She wondered if she could figure out how to spin this as a re-enactment of some ghost story to keep them from leaving bad reviews.

As soon as Billie was close enough, Mitch growled, "Follow him."

"Uh…" She gestured toward the tour group. "Kind of in the middle of something here."

"I'll finish it. Follow him."

"But—"

"*Now.*"

"Shit," Billie muttered, but she did what he said. Mitch had men to be his hired muscle, but her job—her *real* job, when she wasn't pouring drinks or telling fake ghost stories—was to be his eyes. She hurried down the hall and pushed open the heavy door to follow Daniel into the garage. Before the door slammed shut, she heard Mitch magnanimously apologizing to the ghost tour and asking how they were enjoying their stay so far.

On the ground floor of the parking garage, Daniel slammed the door of a crew cab pickup truck, and Billie swore again. She hated shifting in such a public place, but Mitch had left her no choice. She glanced around, confirming no one else was in the garage. If she was quick, no one would see her. Crouching behind a car, she hurriedly shucked out of her clothes, then shoved them behind the fire extinguisher. With an exhale, her body shrank and reformed, folding into her most comfortable animal form: a bobcat. The dark garage lit up as her night vision activated, and the world came alive with smells: the crisscrossing scent trails of everyone who had passed through the garage today, the suffocating exhaust of the vehicles, the rancid trash in the bear-proof bin. Just before Daniel's truck fishtailed out of the garage, Billie darted between the parked cars and leaped into the truck bed.

Wind blew through her fur and she scrambled to keep from sliding around the truck bed as Daniel bumped out onto the road. After a few minutes, she dared to lift her head enough to gauge which direction the truck was going. The Silver Coin was about a mile outside of town, down a steep winding road. The town itself was a cluster of aging houses and historical buildings surrounded by steep peaks and ridges. But Daniel wasn't headed into Juniper. Though Billie lived right off Miners Avenue in the center of town, most people lived along the unpaved or barely-paved roads that snaked around the nearby ridges. It was along one of these that Daniel now drove, turning down a winding gravel road after about half a mile, a "shortcut" that would eventually intersect the closest highway.

If he went too far away from Juniper, Billie would jump out, Mitch and his demands be damned. Juniper was her territory; she couldn't shift outside of it. She wasn't sure exactly what would happen if she passed the edge of her territory. It had been years since she'd left it, even in human form, worried that straying too far from her territory would mean she'd never be able to shift again. In any case, nothing good could come of Daniel getting all the way down to Denver and finding her huddling naked in his truck bed.

But about a mile before Billie was ready to make the leap, Daniel turned down a steep driveway, headlights cutting through the dark pines. He parked, and the truck engine went silent. She waited until the crunch of his boots on gravel turned to the thunk of boots on porch steps before she slipped out of the truck bed and darted into the trees. Glancing back, she recognized Toby Moran's car in the driveway, and that was who came to the door a moment later.

Her claws dug silently into the tree bark and she settled into a crux, spotted front paws draping over the branch. This was a perfect vantage point, and completely out of sight unless the men looked directly at her. And even then, all they would see would be an ordinary, if rather large, bobcat in a tree. That was nothing especially unusual in this mountain community. Less common than the deer and elk that clomped through the middle of town or the coyotes and black bears that scavenged trashcans, but still nothing to get excited about.

"I need more," Daniel said as soon as Toby opened the door. Even from this distance, Billie could smell a waft of something unusual, like a mix of dry red wine and coppery blood. In the porch light, Daniel's face was even more flushed than before. And peeling—like the first layer of his skin had practically burned away. She was somewhat colorblind in bobcat form, with reds and oranges appearing more like greens and blues, but she assumed his face must look unnaturally crimson.

"Shit, man, I'm out," Toby said.

"No," Daniel said—nearly growled.

"You look sunburned as hell, man, are you okay?"

Toby pointed at the skin flaking off of Daniel's arm, but Daniel smacked his hand away and pushed Toby against the wall. "I need more."

"Tomorrow, man. I'm meeting with my supplier tomorrow. Get off me." He pushed Daniel hard enough to send him stumbling backward. "Come on, let's see if I've got anything else that will get you through." Toby disappeared inside, and once Daniel caught his balance, he followed, slamming the door behind him.

Billie climbed down from the tree and circled the cabin. Through the window, she managed to get a glimpse of Toby taking a hit from a large glass bong and Daniel licking residue out of a plastic tube. That was enough to confirm what she'd suspected: Daniel was hooked on Scarlet, and Toby was selling it. That's about all Mitch would need to know.

This was the first hint Billie'd seen of Scarlet being in town. The new synthetic drug had hit the streets of Denver only a couple of months ago and was already proving to be highly addictive and dangerous. Billie figured Mitch wouldn't want his cozy mountain town getting a reputation for it, especially so close to Juniper's biggest tourism day. Or maybe he'd want the revenue from it, and be pissed that Toby had cornered the market. Billie wasn't sure.

Mitch didn't care about all the home brewers who made beer in their bathtubs or distilled whisky in backyard barrels—that was just part of mountain culture. Marijuana was legal in Colorado, and Juniper, small as it was, had both a medical and a recreational store. When it came to anything harder, though, Mitch—who fancied himself the area crime lord—wanted to know where it came from, and wanted a cut of it. He'd threatened Toby a number of times because he'd refused. Like a lot of Juniper's long-term residents, Toby still considered Mitch an outsider, and therefore not to be fully trusted.

She waited a few minutes to see if Daniel would emerge, but after a while Billie peeked back through the window and saw him passed out on the couch. Toby had kicked his feet up onto the cluttered coffee table and turned the TV on. A crime drama played on the screen—that same one Mitch watched obsessively. Nothing more to learn here, then. She padded up to the top of the steep driveway and estimated where she was. Daniel had driven several miles through the winding mountain roads, but if she trekked straight through the forest, she could probably get back to the Silver Coin in just under an hour. A little longer if she stopped by her cave first, which seemed like a good idea. Shifting there was far preferable to taking the risk of someone seeing her in the parking garage, not to mention the awkwardness of trying to get dressed while hiding behind some tourist's rental car. Assuming no one had found her clothes and stuffed them into the hotel's lost and found. She darted across the road.

Her cat's-eye night vision let her navigate the dark forest quickly and smoothly. Though these days she mostly used her shifting ability at Mitch's command, there was still a joy to being able to run through the forest in animal form. She felt so much lighter, so much more at home in her skin as a bobcat. She scaled a tumble of boulders and leaped across a stream. A deer started at her sudden appearance and crashed off through the trees, first flashing wide eyes, then white tail in the filtered moonlight. She crossed a couple of empty roads, and accidentally tripped the motion sensor light at a newly-built cabin. At a stone outcropping a quarter-mile from the Silver Coin, she used her teeth to tug a grass mat away from a gap between two rock faces. It kept her cave from being noticed by off-trail hikers or forest service workers.

Inside the cave, she shape-shifted back into human form. White-blue light from her small camping lamp filled the cave; she always kept it there so she could find her clothes once she switched back to the dulled night vision of her human senses. A spider had strung a fresh partial web from the button of her spare jeans to the cave wall. She swept it off and shook out all her clothes, checking for inhabitants before she pulled them on. One of her sleeves had torn loose of its hem, so she sat shirtless on the ground, dug her sewing kit out of the box and quickly sewed it back up. She inspected it: not as precise as her machine would have done, but passable. Fully dressed, she brushed her hair and applied some lipstick, the only makeup she ever wore, and stashed the brush back into her supply box. An animal went into the cave and a woman emerged. Time to go back to the Silver Coin Hotel and tell Mitch what she had seen.

It was much slower going in human form, but she knew this path well, even in the dark. By the time she walked through the hotel's front doors, the big antique clock in the lobby showed it was after midnight. The ghost tour was long over, and the bar was vacant. One night clerk, Kim, sat behind the front desk. She glanced up, gave Billie a perfunctory wave, and went back to whatever game she was playing on the hotel computer. A couple of lightbulbs were burnt out on the lobby's elk antler chandelier, and Billie noticed the taxidermied bear was in need of dusting.

She retrieved her clothes from the parking garage first, and stuffed them into her cubby behind the bar. Then she went into the elevator, keying in the special code that would take her to Mitch's secret casino on the top floor. Most Western states only had casinos on tribal land, but Colorado's laws allowed a few historical mining towns to run them: Black Hawk, Cripple Creek, and Central City. Juniper was a historical mining town too, but the games Mitch hosted on the top floor of the Silver Coin Hotel were unregulated and off the radar. Juniper was small enough that it had no local police, and Billie assumed that Mitch had bribed whoever he needed to in neighboring jurisdictions to look the other way. Legal casinos all had computerized machines now, so Mitch had bought up a whole bunch of the old pull lever slot machines. It created a more authentic atmosphere than simply having a few illicit card games, he said. Though they certainly had plenty of those as well.

The elevator opened, and the lively atmosphere of the casino was a stark contrast to the empty ground floor. The chairs in front of the slot machines were nearly all occupied, a mix of a few dozen locals and tourists who had been vouched for by some friend of a friend. The high rollers at the craps table smacked their hands against the table as the dice came up bad. Used shot glasses and empty bottles piled up on bistro tables. Cigar smoke curled above a poker table, and Billie wrinkled her nose at the smell. She crossed to the far side of the casino floor and tapped on the door of Mitch's office. Once the security lights above the handle flashed green, she pushed it open and entered.

Mitch shut a laptop with a snap.

"So," he said before she'd even closed the door. "What did my favorite kitty cat find out tonight?"

She hated it when he called her that. He did it in front of everyone, too. In addition to the undercurrent of sexual harassment, this nickname also carried the implicit threat that he could expose her shapeshifting abilities to people who had no business knowing that kind of thing about her. He'd said it more frequently ever since the one time she'd asked him not to.

As she told him what she'd seen, Mitch leaned back in his chair, swiveling side to side. Then he brought himself to a sudden stop and pointed at her. "What's it been, five years you've worked here?"

"Closer to six," Billie said.

"Six years," he said. He looked up at the ceiling as though he were reminiscing. Billie cleared her throat to reclaim his attention. Mitch snapped his fingers and leaned forward, leveling his gaze at her. "I've got a new job for you."

"Okay," she said.

"I'll pay you more for this one. It will require your special talent."

Mitch stared at a spot in the air just to her left, tapping his index finger knuckle to his lips in thought. Billie pointed to the door. "I can come back when you get around to spitting out whatever it is you want from me."

He dropped his hand, smiled facetiously at her, and started swiveling his chair again. Billie found the habit maddening, but then, there were few things about Mitch that didn't irritate her. "Toby Moran's been a pain in my ass for years now," Mitch said. "Hell, he's been a pain in the ass of this whole town. I can think of lots of people who would be just as happy as I would if Toby just suddenly… disappeared."

Billie frowned. "How do you mean?"

"Well, you know out where he lives is so rural and wild. I doubt anyone would be too surprised if Toby met his unfortunate end from a wild animal attack."

Billie hesitated, letting her mind process the request. Her chest suddenly tightened.

"I'm not a murderer, Mitch."

He waved his hand. "Murder," he said. "Such a nasty word. Think of it as pest control. You'd be doing this town a favor."

"You're not serious."

He *couldn't* be serious. Mitch might like to act like he was the Tony Soprano of the Rockies, but he was really only a petty criminal, and Billie was pretty sure he'd never actually ordered a hit or killed anyone. He had two goons, Frankie and Gil, who were happy to throw punches on his behalf, but black eyes and broken noses were about as brutal as anything got. As far as she knew.

"Totally serious," he said, with a wink that didn't clarify the situation at all.

Billie shook her head. "What if I just steal the Scarlet when Toby brings it home tomorrow? *That* I can do."

"This isn't about the drugs," Mitch said. "It's about how much easier my life is going to be without that fucking weasel in it anymore. Just shift into a bear and give him a big hug. It'll be easy."

"I can't."

"Like I said, it's not—"

"No, I mean, I can't shift into a bear. It's too big." She understood how her shifting worked about as well as she understood how her liver worked, but she did know that somehow she could manage to shift into forms that were smaller than her human body, but not bigger. It was a type of folding, her mother had always said. If she *could* manage a bear, it wouldn't be a very intimidating one.

"How about a lion?" Mitch suggested.

"Mountain lion?"

*Mom's shape,* Billie couldn't help but think. She'd always promised one day she'd teach Billie how to find it. But now she wasn't here to keep any of those old promises. And if she were, she certainly wouldn't approve of how Mitch was asking her to use her power.

"Of course a mountain lion," Mitch said. "Circus lion would be far more suspicious. Though it would make a more interesting news story, for sure. No such thing as bad publicity. Can you do a circus lion?"

Billie shook her head, disgusted that she'd even given it that much thought. "No. And I'm not going to kill Toby Moran."

Mitch grinned at her. "Eh, it was worth a shot." He flipped open his laptop again. "Well, looks like I'll have to have yet another chat with Mr. Moran about his business interests in this town."

Billie hesitated, and after a moment Mitch looked up from his desk and waved her away, saying, "You can go." Then, before she shut the door, he added, "And tell that worthless son of mine you live with that his payment is late." Billie sighed and closed the door behind her.

It was close to three in the morning by the time Billie made it home and crawled into bed. She slinked a hand over Caleb's shoulder, kissed the wing of his shoulder blade. He rolled over and scooped her into the crook of his arm. She nuzzled against his chest.

"You shifted tonight, didn't you?" he said, the words lazy with sleep.

"How can you tell?"

He twined his fingers into her hair. "You always smell like pine trees after you shift."

She tilted her head up to kiss him, starting soft, becoming more urgent. They broke apart, and her lips brushed the stubble on his cheek. She swept strands of light brown hair away from his forehead. It was just long enough to fall into his eyes.

"I've forgotten what you look like," she whispered.

He rolled her on top of him, and she pressed the length of her body against his, as much of their skin touching as she could manage.

The whispered words were rehashed from a fight they'd had a few weeks back, but had morphed, somehow, into a phrase of endearment. This space in the middle of the night was sometimes the only time they had together. Billie worked afternoons and evenings at the Silver Coin, and Caleb got up at five to work at the quarry. She had tried several times to align their schedules, but Mitch had always found reasons why he needed her to work nights.

It *was* true that her shapeshifting came in handy more often under the cover of night. Most of the spying tasks Mitch sent her on revolved around personal drama. A parent who wanted to know where the teenagers really went on Friday night, a husband who suspected a cheating wife. It was never the other way around; though there were plenty of cheating husbands in Juniper, the women generally didn't go to Mitch when they wanted answers. Sometimes her job was to make sure whoever gambled in Mitch's illegal casino didn't leave town when they owed him something. But it was clear he was keeping Billie and Caleb apart on purpose. Another way to punish Caleb for not being who Mitch had wanted him to be, justified by Mitch claiming this was what he paid her for.

That Mitch paid her at all was kind of a joke, since Billie had found herself caught in the middle of Mitch and Caleb's feud. Half of what Caleb earned working at the quarry went to Mitch—essentially a student loan payment, since Mitch had paid Caleb's way through college with the agreement that Caleb would come work for him once he had his business degree. But at some point, Caleb had changed his major and decided he wanted nothing to do with his dad's illicit dealings or tourist traps, so Mitch had treated him just like anyone else who owed him a debt, going psuedo-mob boss on him and demanding repayment, with interest. Since Billie worked for Mitch and lived with Caleb, the money Caleb paid came right back to them in a weird circle. She tried not to think about how that meant she was basically working for free. But what else could she do? Juniper was her territory, and she couldn't leave it, or she risked losing the power to shapeshift. They were trapped, and though the cycle was obnoxious, at least it was stable.

Billie clung to Caleb as he moved beneath her, wishing she could prolong every second, wishing she could preserve this sense of freedom she felt when there was no one else around but the two of them, those moments completely free of fear that she only found in his arms. Billie avoided even casual touch with most people, choosing not to shake hands or return a friendly hug unless it was especially awkward not to. But with Caleb, she could not get enough of his touch. His hand fell absently away from her onto the bed and she lifted it back up to her skin, relishing the sensations as he rubbed his hands up and down her back.

After, Caleb fell back to sleep and Billie lay awake, staring up at the shadows of the tree branches on the ceiling until the sunrise began to paint the sky orange. The conversation with Mitch replayed through her mind. How could he ask something so terrible of her so casually? And how could she have even given it a moment's thought?

# MONDAY

Caleb watched the rise and fall of Billie's breath in the dim morning light. Sometimes, when she seemed so relaxed and peaceful like this, he imagined scooping her up, blankets and all, and carrying her out to the car, and then driving until this town was far behind them. She'd be mad when she first woke up, but soon she'd realize that they were free.

He'd never do it, of course. She said she couldn't leave town, said she'd lose a vital piece of herself if she did. *He'd* left for a while, gone down to Boulder for college. But even then, he'd called her nearly every day, talking for long hours when he should have been studying for his next test or out at parties on The Hill. He bragged to his friends that he was dating "an older girl"—which was technically true since Billie was a year older than him—and that she was into really kinky stuff—less true, but a way his nineteen-year-old brain had rationalized the fact that his girlfriend sometimes turned into a literal wildcat. When he'd graduated and she still wouldn't leave Juniper to join him, he'd come back here to be with her.

He kissed her temple and left her sleeping. He pulled on clean clothes, knowing they would be grimy and stained within a couple of hours. The coffee he brewed was stronger than he really cared for, but

16

he dumped the whole pot into a thermos. The quarry was about the only place he could work that didn't mean either an hour-plus commute or working at his dad's hotel. Moving back to Juniper had meant admitting to his dad that he had switched his major to geology, instead of getting the business degree they'd agreed on. He told himself that working at the quarry was somewhat related to his degree, but it really wasn't. It was grunt work, blasting and hauling rock, all sweat and muscle. But it meant he could be with Billie.

His phone buzzed; Brock was there to pick him up. But as Caleb glanced at the message, he noticed a missed call from late the previous night. It was from Jennifer, a girl he'd known in Boulder, someone he'd had a brief fling with. *Weird*, he thought. He hadn't even talked to her in over two years, had tried to leave all that behind.

During his sophomore year, the strain of being apart had begun to weigh on them, and Caleb's friends ridiculed him, claiming he'd made Billie up, since she refused to visit Boulder. He'd decided after taking Intro Psychology that Billie's refusal to leave Juniper was probably a type of agoraphobia related to the trauma of her mother's death. He sympathized—he'd lost his own mom, too—but his friends' teasing and his own frustration outweighed his sympathies. He started messing around with other girls, and although a few of his flings were enjoyable, they were mostly just for show. He never felt a real connection with those Boulder girls with their yoga pants and ski passes and lower back tattoos. He never felt the same spark when he touched them, that same overwhelming urge to both protect and be protected by them. And he regretted those affairs, didn't want his past mistakes bubbling up again to mess up the little time he now got with Billie. He swiped the notification away.

Outside, Caleb shoved some trash under the seat of Brock's car to make room for his legs, and slammed the door shut behind him.

"Morning, dawg," Brock said and handed him a joint.

Caleb took one long draw and handed it back to Brock, waving it away the next time Brock passed it over. One hit was just enough.

Just enough to stave off the ache in his back he still felt from last Friday; just enough to make the foreman's bullshit funny instead of irritating; just enough to get through another long morning. Brock drove through the small town, up into the mountain, and down along the other side of Juniper Ridge, where big machines steadily chipped away at the limestone and marble. They loaded those broken pieces into trucks that drove them somewhere far away.

At lunch break, Jennifer called again. Caleb took a bite of his soggy sandwich and stared at the screen. Her picture was an old one from their college days, a duck-face selfie she'd drunk-texted him one night, trying to convince him to come over to her dorm. He should probably just block her. He didn't need Billie seeing this and getting the wrong idea. But he swiped to answer.

"Hey, thought I told you not to call me," he said.

"Caleb? Oh my god, okay. Have you heard from Madison?"

"What? No, I don't ever talk to any of that crew anymore." Occasionally he saw the odd Instagram post, but he had no idea what had become of most of his college friends. Madison had been a couple of years younger, was probably still in school.

"Shit. Okay. You're still up in the mountains?"

"Yeah."

"There's been some weird stuff happening down here. I think... I think Madison might have joined a cult."

"Um."

"Just, if you hear from her, or from anyone else, let me know? I'm hoping I'm wrong."

"Sure," Caleb said.

"I'll let you know when I find out for sure where she is."

*Don't bother*, Caleb wanted to say. He didn't want to get drawn into drama with a bunch of people he used to drink with. Jennifer had been alright as far as the girls he'd known, but he'd left that whole life behind. Not that he wished murderous cults on any of them, but he didn't see what all this had to do with him.

"Yeah, thanks," he said, and hung up.

"Who's the side chick?" Brock asked. "Is she hot?"

"Nobody," Caleb said, and stuffed the rest of his sandwich into his mouth. "And no."

"I ain't gonna tell Billie, dawg."

"It's not like that," Caleb said again, mouth still full. He balled up the aluminum foil and tossed it at Brock, who tried to karate chop it in the air. Back to work, so he could forget all about Jennifer and Madison and the others. So he could maybe get off in time to see Billie for a few minutes before she was gone again.

Mid-morning, after not nearly enough sleep, Billie dragged herself out of bed to go answer the banging at the door. She shucked on jeans and rubbed the crust out of her eyes. It was probably another lost tourist who had mistaken her house for the dispensary or teashop—it was a risk of living right on the Miners Avenue, and she'd come home more than once to strangers sitting on her porch "waiting for her to open." Billie yanked open the door, ready to tell them to get lost, but stopped short when she saw who was actually standing there.

The man on her porch was balding, with thin gray wisps hanging desperately onto a pale scalp. Thick bags puffed under each eye. He was very thin, but his arms were muscular and deeply suntanned. He wore a black t-shirt with a couple of holes in the sleeve, faded jeans, and brown cowboy boots. He smiled at her, light blue eyes looking wistful.

"Billie," he said. "Baby doll, I'm home."

"No," Billie said, coming to her senses after the shock of seeing the man she had never expected to see again. Certainly never *wanted* to see again. She tried to slam the door but he caught it just before it shut. Her voice came out strained. "You are not welcome here."

"Billie, I know you think you hate me, but please, let's just talk."

"I'm calling Mitch," Billie said. He didn't drop his hand from the door, didn't back away. That threat would have been plenty for most people in Juniper, but Billie realized her father might not even know who Mitch was. The Silver Coin Hotel had still been a vacant historic dancehall when he was arrested thirteen years ago—Mitch and Caleb had arrived in town three years later.

"I'll call the police," she tried instead.

He let go. She shut the door and turned the deadbolt. Then she went and checked the windows, and the back door as well. When she came back, he was still outside, still talking to her through the door.

"—going to sit here until you come out and talk to me," he was saying.

Billie sank down on the inside of the door, knees to her chest. About a year ago, she had denied three collect calls from the prison, thrown out two letters without even opening them. She should have known the increased frequency meant he was nearing release, but she had refused to believe they would ever let the monster walk free again. She should have been prepared. Should have known he'd come back here eventually.

He was still talking, saying something about how much he had loved her mother. Billie scrambled to her feet. She had to get away from him. Quietly, she crept to the back door and eased it open, wincing at the creak of the screen door. She squeezed through the broken fence in the backyard and slipped into the vacant livery stable next door. It had been abandoned for years, and Billie kept a stash of clothes there, like in her cave over by the hotel. She stripped quickly and added the clothes to the pile. Her keys and phone had been left in the cabin, and this meant she'd be stuck without them for the day, but it was a worthy sacrifice. Her human form melted away and the familiar fur of her bobcat form wrapped her like a comforting blanket. She stuck her head out the stable's back door, looking and sniffing, and when she was confident the coast was clear, she ran, leaping over the fence, darting through a neighbor's yard. Over the creek and up the hill toward Juniper Ridge, her cave awaited, a safe space her dad had never known about.

Billie had been shapeshifting as long as she could walk, but her mother had told her from the very beginning that it had to stay a secret from everyone but the two of them.

"It's a private thing," she had always said. "People will get mad. They'll be jealous that they can't shift too, and they'll try to take it away from us. Even Daddy. He'd be the maddest of all."

Her dad had never hurt her, though Billie had seen him get in fights with other men, often over trifling things, and sometimes he drank so much that he passed out on the kitchen table or slumped halfway off the couch. It was often on those nights that she and her mother would go out into the forest together.

But one night, when Billie was twelve, they left their clothes on the back porch and ran through the forest, a small bobcat and a mountain lion. They sprinted through the forest, climbing trees, stalking deer, and when they got back, neither of them saw Billie's father sitting on the porch. Billie stopped at the edge of the trees to scratch her ear, and she was three strokes into the scratch when she heard the shotgun. She looked up to see her mother, the great beautiful lioness, lying on her side with a shotgun blast through her chest. Slowly, with none of the normal grace of a shift, the body unfolded and transformed back into the form of a woman, her torso a mess of motionless gore.

Billie was back in her human form before she even realized she'd shifted, and she ran to her mother, a piercing child's scream echoing against the mountains. Her father stood on the back porch with the gun still in his hands. His face betrayed a look of utter shock and for a moment he didn't move while Billie wailed. Then he grabbed Billie by her hair and shoved her into the house. With trembling fingers, she managed to call 911. Blood from her mother's body smeared onto the white cordless phone. When the police arrived, they found her father in the backyard staring at the body. He didn't resist arrest or try to spin any kind of excuse.

Billie had been forced to repeat what happened to half a dozen police officers, but she remembered how adamant her mother had been that no one know their secret, so she made up a story about how she'd been sleepwalking and her mom had come outside to stop her from wandering into the forest. It was the only thing she could think of that might justify why they'd both been nude at the time, and she was pretty sure they didn't entirely believe her. At least she had been spared having to sit in on the trial in Denver, though she couldn't escape all the local whispers, reporting various versions of what was happening in the court: that her father had remorselessly pled guilty to everything; that he'd been convicted of child molestation as well as murder; that they'd linked him to a decade-old string of killings in Colorado Springs; that he'd tried to blame the death on some imaginary cousin. Fortunately, the story that he'd thought he was shooting at a mountain lion instead of a woman got mixed up in all the other rumors, and no one seemed to take it seriously, so Billie's secret remained safe.

Billie had moved out of her childhood home on Shadow Ridge and gone to live with her grandmother in the cabin on Miners Avenue, where she still lived. Her grandmother was her father's mother; she had no contact with her mother's family. Didn't even know who they were, or where they were. Billie's grandmother never spoke about what her son had done except for once, just before she died, when she went on a long rant about the power of forgiveness, which Billie had summarily dismissed.

At school, a few of the girls spread the rumor that Billie's mother had been a witch. That was the reason she'd been naked when she was shot, they said, she'd been out in the forest dancing with the devil and Billie's father had just been doing the Lord's work and ridding the town of evil. Billie threw enough punches to get herself suspended from school twice, and spent as much of her adolescence out of human form as she could manage, stalking the edges of her territory, never quite brave enough to venture very far beyond where she thought her boundaries were. Losing her mother had been bad enough; she couldn't risk losing the unique gift her mother had given her. She would disappear into the forest for whole days sometimes, and wondered if she could live a whole life that way. Until she got to know Caleb, who had also lost his mother, who didn't believe any of the mean things the other teens said about her, who made her, at least occasionally, glad to be in human form.

By the time she made it to the cave, Billie felt all that history weighing on her, the aching absence of her mother, thirteen years of rage toward her father. She let out a caterwaul that echoed against the cave walls, then unfolded to human form and sat on the cold stone floor with her head in her hands, wanting to cry but not even sure she could.

"How about a lion?" Mitch's request echoed in her mind. She wouldn't profane her mother's preferred shape by turning herself into Mitch's weapon, but using those teeth and claws to avenge her mother was a different story. Maybe if she could get her dad alone and be sure he was unarmed, she could shift into that terrifying form, make him understand that he was not welcome here.

A mountain lion should have been an accessible form for her now, as the animal was closer to her human weight than the bobcat form she was so comfortable with. When she was a kid, she could sometimes shift into smaller mammals such as a housecat or a raccoon, but she couldn't remember the last time she'd even tried to use those forms. Anything non-mammal had always been impossible, as was anything that weighed more than her human form did. It wasn't an exact conservation of mass, but there were definite limits on what she could manage. A pretty narrow window, really, and it was in bobcat form that she felt most compact, most in control. Maybe if her mother hadn't died, Billie had always thought, then she could have learned to expand beyond that window, or gain better control of different forms.

But then, her mother was also the reason Billie had never tried to shift into a mountain lion before. That form had gotten her killed. People didn't tend to fear a bobcat unless it was lurking around their chicken coop, but mountain lions they treated like monsters.

*Well*, she thought, rage filling her again, *maybe a monster is the only thing that can fight off another monster.*

Her body heated up in preparation for a shift and she took all of that sadness and rage with her into the form, willing herself into the shape of the lion. The shift finished and she looked down to see the same spotted legs she always had. Still just a bobcat. Billie sat on her haunches and cleaned her fur. This was just the way it was.

Billie stayed in her cave until she became restless, then got dressed and headed in to the Silver Coin early. One of the desk clerks caught her as soon as she walked in to let her know Caleb had called asking about her. Billie's heart sank. This was one of the few days when they were supposed to be able to have an early dinner together in the narrow gap between when he got home from the quarry and she left for the hotel. She used the front desk phone to call him back and ask him to bring her phone and wallet over.

She was eating a burger at the bar when he got there, and though she hoped he'd stay and eat with her, he handed her the stuff, kissed her, and tried to take off right away. Billie barely had time to let him know that her dad was back in town and looking for her. He hesitated, clearly torn between wanting to stay and offer her comfort and protection, and not wanting to cross paths with his own dad.

"I'm safe here," she assured him, and he kissed her again, a little deeper this time, then left as quickly as he could, glancing over his shoulder to make sure he got out before Mitch saw him.

Just after Caleb left, Mitch passed through. Not even commenting on the fact she was there two hours early, he rapped his knuckles on the bar and said, "Text me when Toby gets here."

*Toby?* Billie had practically forgotten about the drama from the night before. Apparently, Mitch had arranged for another pressure-chat with Juniper's rogue drug dealer. She wondered if this one would do any more good than previous attempts. Mitch held a lot of sway in the town, but some of the residents who had grown up here still resented the way he'd blown in to town a decade ago and decided he ran the place.

Once she finished eating, Billie carried her own dishes back to the tiny kitchen, then clocked in and planted herself on the other side of the bar. No customers were there yet, just Frankie and Gil, Mitch's two henchmen, arguing in the corner booth over a soccer game that played on the one small television screen. The two of them had moved to Juniper a few years ago, and she'd never seen one without the other.

It wouldn't take much asking around to track her here, but if her dad came looking for her at the Silver Coin, then he *would* become Mitch's problem. Frankie and Gil cared nothing about her personally, but she worked for Mitch, so they'd stand up for her.

As late afternoon stretched into evening, Billie poured drinks for locals and hotel patrons alike, holding her breath each time the lobby doors opened.

Around 6:00, the doors burst open, but it still wasn't Billie's dad who entered. Instead, a woman in a short dress and high heels clacked in to the bar. Robyn Applebaum. Billie groaned. On any other day, she would easily say this was the last person in the world she wanted to see.

Robyn and Billie had been in the same grade in school, and she'd been one of those who professed loudly, and often, that Billie's mother had been a witch. Juniper was hardly large enough for a school on its own, but the town was centrally located enough that children from half a dozen other small mountain communities were bussed in. Most of them, she'd never seen again after high school. But Robyn had stuck around, determined—like Mitch—to revitalize the old mining town. She sold real estate and managed most of the vacation rentals in the area, and was one of the organizers of the big Fourth of July festival coming up next weekend.

"Just out looking for a Monday night party?" Billie snarked as she poured the fruity drink Robyn ordered.

"I'm meeting with clients, of course," Robyn said in a faux-cheerful tone. "Lovely couple from Centennial, tired of the metro rat-race and looking for a nice peaceful mountain home. They're staying up here for the week, I'm sure we'll close on something soon."

"How good for you," Billie said flatly. Chances were the couple would get scared out after their first real mountain winter and Robyn would be able to sell it again next year. Or else they'd use it two weeks out of the year and rent it to a rotating queue of tourists the rest of the time, with Robyn taking care of the upkeep and getting a cut of each rental. That's how these deals usually went.

"Well thank you!" Robyn replied, with no indication she understood Billie's sarcasm. She leaned closer. "Now, I was thinking about that offer I told you about, and—"

"I'm not selling." Billie pushed the drink toward her. This conversation wasn't new, and Billie's answer hadn't changed.

Robyn sighed. "I *really* wish you'd reconsider. I have a developer who's motivated to buy, but they want the whole lot." That meant Billie's cabin as well as the abandoned building next to it. The last time she'd accosted Billie, Robyn had stressed that it was an all or nothing deal: both Billie's cabin and the vacant livery stable. They wouldn't buy one without the other. Billie had no interest in losing either.

"I inherited that house," Billie said. "My grandfather built it with his own hands. I'm not going to sell it so you can tear it down and build a strip mall."

It wasn't that Billie had any sentimental attachment to it as a family home. She hadn't even known her grandfather, who had apparently drank himself to death before she was born, and she'd had a somewhat frosty relationship with her grandmother. The cabin was tiny, with no closets, and only had a wood stove, which left it freezing in the winter. But her grandmother had willed it to Billie when she died, and it was a huge relief not to have to worry about rent or mortgage on her limited income. Besides that, Billie didn't know where she would go if she did sell. There weren't many houses in town that Robyn hadn't already remodeled into fancy vacation homes. Billie couldn't afford another local house, and she wouldn't be able to shift anymore if she left Juniper. That was a part of herself she wasn't willing to give up, even if it meant being stuck in this crappy town forever.

Robyn huffed. "It's not going to be a strip mall." She snatched the drink, tilting it dangerously close to spilling. But then she cut short whatever other admonitions were burning on her tongue, and waved to the couple who had just come down the stairs. The same ones, Billie realized, who had been in the ghost tour yesterday. Robyn turned back to Billie for a moment and whispered, "You are single-handedly holding this town back from reaching its full potential."

The woman gave Billie a confused glance as she approached the bar, but her voice stayed chipper. "Oh, hey! From the ghost tour, right?"

"Uh, yeah," Billie said, a bit surprised the woman recognized her. In her experience, tourists tended to have a very short memory when it came to local faces. "Sorry it didn't go well. I'm not usually the one who leads them."

"No problem," the woman said. "But that man you chased after—he looked like he was having a heart attack. Is he okay?"

"Daniel? Yeah. I think so, anyway."

"Oh, good, I've been so worried. I'm Chloe, by the way." She extended a hand covered in rings and bracelets. Not expensive jewelry: a string of rose quartz around her wrist and common polished gemstones in silver settings on her fingers. Most of it looked like the trinkets the tourist shops sold.

Billie raised her hands and said, "Sorry, bit sticky from the Coke dispenser. But I'm Billie."

"Oh!" Chloe dropped her hand, but the smile stayed on her face. "No problem. Nice to meet you, Billie."

"If you're interested in ghosts," Billie said as she pretended to clean the syrup off her fingers, "I recommend going to the Enchanted Mountain Metaphysical Shop on Miners Avenue and talking to Heather. She knows the real stories."

Chloe's smile grew bigger. "I think I'll do that. Thanks!"

Robyn cleared her throat, and Chloe shouted over to the table where Robyn and the man were sitting down. "Luke, what do you want?" Then waved a hand before he could answer and said, "Nevermind, he never gets anything except a Coors Light. And give me something that looks like alcohol, but isn't."

"I'll have those right out," Billie said, already filling the first frosted mug. Chloe joined the other two. Robyn plopped a big red binder on the table and started flipping through, talking about the houses they could go see.

Billie carried the drinks over to the table. Robyn didn't move the binder to make space for the drinks until Billie cleared her throat.

Chloe was busy listing off all the adventures they had planned for the next day, starting with an early morning hike on one of the newest National Forest trails.

"We can go out looking on Wednesday afternoon instead," Robyn said. "That's fine. Here, I think this should be one of the first properties we look at." As Billie set the glass down in front of Chloe, she glanced at the sheet Robyn was showing them, and her throat tightened. Shadow Ridge. She didn't need to read the full address to recognize the red stained wood siding and the small brick garden plot in the front yard. This was the house where Billie had lived as a child. Where her mother had died. Did Robyn know?

Billie stood there long enough that all three of them looked up at her.

"Thanks, we don't need anything else right now," Chloe said, raising the drink to her lips. Billie searched Robyn's face for any indication that she knew, that she had chosen that property to show them just to torment Billie, but Robyn only smiled and kept on telling the couple how they would just *love* the remodeled kitchen.

Hours later, her father hadn't tracked her to the hotel, but Toby hadn't shown up either. Mitch fumed down to the bar and pulled Billie into the hallway.

"Go find that asshole and bring him back here so we can have our little chat."

"Wouldn't Frankie and Gil be better for this?" Billie hooked a thumb toward the booth where the two of them had been hanging out, though they'd headed upstairs about an hour ago.

"They are… otherwise engaged at the moment. What, you don't think you can handle one lazy drug dealer?"

"Can I take your truck?" At Mitch's scowl, she said, "Well, I can't very well bring him back without a vehicle, can I?"

"You can bring me his head, for all I care."

Billie closed her eyes, took a deep breath, and bit back a few choice words. Managing to sound calmer than she felt, she said, "Can I please borrow your truck? I don't have the car tonight, and this isn't the kind of job I can do on foot."

Meaning, they both knew, that she would be going as a person, not as a bobcat, unless some kind of self-defense or quick escape necessitated a shift. The car was back at home, and Caleb was likely asleep by now. Even if he wasn't, if he knew it was a favor for Mitch, he wouldn't bring it.

Mitch dug in his pocket and shoved keys at her. "You scratch the paint and you're instantly demoted to housekeeper pay."

"Yeah, 'cause you're such the careful driver." Before Mitch could snap anything back, she raised her hands, keys dangling from an index finger. "I'll drive like an old lady, I promise. And I'll be back with Toby as soon as I can."

Mitch's truck was a black beast that Billie practically needed a step ladder to climb into. The four-door cab alone was as long as her car. A metal toolbox took up a quarter of the bed area, and he had a tarp and some trash bags in the rest of it. Billie yanked on the seat levers, trying to adjust the driver's seat for her smaller frame.

On a hunch, she drove into town first. She glanced at the windows of her cabin as she passed by. Dark. So Caleb was asleep after all. Their shared car waited out front. She parked in front of Fred's Bar and Grill on Miners Avenue before venturing all the way out to Toby's house. If he wasn't at home, he was likely here, and she might just save herself a trip.

Fred's was moderately full for a Monday night. She peered around but didn't see Toby, and when she asked the bartender if he'd been in recently, he told her, "No, but someone's been looking for you." He pointed to a corner table, where her dad sat with a glass beer bottle and an empty burger basket.

"Shit." Billie turned, but it was too late. He'd seen her. He stood so fast he nearly knocked his drink off of the table.

She got outside as quickly as she could, but he caught her arm before she reached the truck. She yanked it out of his grasp.

"Billie, please. I'm your father."

She rounded on him. "*No.* You lost the right to that title the day you decided to put a bullet in my mother."

"It was an accident, Billie. You know it was. If I'd known that she, that she could—"

Billie held her hands up. She looked around and lowered her voice. "Stop. You're not going around here telling people that story, are you?"

"I just—"

"Do you know how much danger you're putting *me* in by telling people that?"

"I didn't—"

"Why did you even come back here?"

He laughed. Actually *laughed*, and Billie's anger rose another several decibels. "This is my home," he said.

She couldn't deny that, as much as she wanted to. Billie lived in the house her father's father had built, and she knew that his father before him had settled here to work the silver mine before Juniper was even an official town. It was her mother who had been the outsider.

"Fine." Billie backed away. "But you stay the hell away from me, and you keep my mother's name and her abilities off of your lips."

She climbed into Mitch's truck and slammed the door before he could say anything else, and drove in the direction Daniel had the night before to go track down Toby.

Billie didn't see anything unusual as she drove down Toby's steep driveway to park in front of his house, but she smelled the blood as soon as she stepped out of the truck. The sharp copper of hemoglobin and the lemon stink of adrenaline: the leftover stench of confused fear, strong enough that even her human senses could pick it up.

A body lay lifeless on the gravel a few feet from the front porch. Was that Toby? It was hard to tell under the mess of gore. She stared in shock for a moment, and then reeled back, running before she even realized she was moving. After a few strides into the forest, once the pine overpowered the blood scent in the air, she stopped and leaned against a tree trunk.

The grief of seeing her mother's corpse surged up from her

memory so strong that she lost sight of the present moment, and was back in that yard with the smell of the shotgun powder, her child-screams echoing off the mountain peaks. She shook her head, the sound of her own heartbeat loud in her ears. She pushed herself away from the tree, swallowing the bile, and made herself walk back to the driveway.

This wasn't a shotgun blast, or any kind of weapon wound. Toby's face had three massive scratches across it, and it looked like something had eaten his stomach, leaving severed bits of intestine trailing out onto the gravel. It appeared to be a wild animal attack, just like Mitch had asked for.

But then, since she hadn't done it, who had?

Billie fumbled for her phone, flipped it open, and found Mitch's number with trembling fingers.

Mitch picked up after a couple of rings, his voice irritated. "What?"

"He's, Toby, he's, um. We have a problem."

"I don't care what his problem is, you bring him to me."

"No, he's, um. He's dead. It looks like an animal attack."

Mitch paused for a moment, and then he laughed so loudly Billie had to pull the phone away from her ear. "I knew you had it in you," he said, still guffawing.

"No!" Billie quieted her voice, suddenly aware of how far sound could carry in the mountains. "I—he was like this when I got here, I swear. Mitch, what do we do?"

The phone was briefly muffled as he talked to someone else. Then he was back, saying, "Just stay there. Make sure no one else sees it."

"Wait, how am I supposed to do that? Mitch, what…?"

But he had hung up. Billie shoved the phone back into her pocket and walked in a circle, wringing her hands. Finally, she shut off Mitch's truck, leaving the keys in the ignition, and went to hide behind the trees. If anyone did come, they'd see Mitch's vehicle, not hers. She could run. There was nothing to connect her to this death.

It probably *was* a mountain lion. A real one. Just a coincidence. An impeccably-timed coincidence.

An agonizing fifteen minutes later, headlights streamed down the driveway and a black car pulled to a stop behind Mitch's truck. Billie stayed in the trees until she saw Frankie and Gil step out, then she rushed out to meet them.

Gil squatted down next to the body, letting out a long, low whistle. Frankie told Billie, "Boss wants us to get whatever money and drugs he's got in his cabin, and take them back to the Silver Coin."

"What about…"

He tossed a pair of latex gloves at her. They fell to the ground and she blinked at them for a moment before the image made any sense to her. Fingerprints, she realized. If she was going to be prowling through the home of a dead man, they didn't want her to be leaving fingerprints all over. Numbly, she leaned over and picked the gloves up.

She really didn't know Frankie and Gil very well, and she wondered if they had past experience cleaning up crime scenes, or if, like Mitch, they took all their cues from TV crime shows. Would they get rid of the body, or just leave it lying there? She should have turned the truck around and left the whole scene alone as soon as she saw what had happened.

Toby's screen door was swinging in the breeze. The keys dangled from the door handle, the door not quite unlocked. A trail of blood splashed across the porch, as though he'd been attacked on his way inside. Billie nudged the door open with her foot and carefully stepped through. Frankie and Gil followed her in and brushed right past her as though they knew exactly where they were going. They plopped an open duffle bag on the couch.

The coffee table was littered with beer cans, half-smoked joints, ash-filled pipes, and two ounces of marijuana, one in a clear baggie, the other in a brown paper sack with the local dispensary logo on it.

But it took a little more digging to find the other stuff. In a closet, she found a suitcase of prescription pills and a few bags of some white powder, which she added to the duffle bag. In the bathroom, she discovered a stash of rubber-banded money behind the toilet. She held the rolls for a moment, wondering if Mitch would let her keep it if she told him she'd been the one who killed Toby. But then, if she told him she'd done this, how many other horrible things would he ask her to do? She couldn't fake it a second time.

Frankie and Gil had uncovered a bunch of other rolls of money and added them to the bag. In the refrigerator, Billie found a tray of red-purple tubes. The Scarlet, freshly delivered. These shouldn't go in the duffle bag, she reasoned. They might break and leak all over everything. She started to carry the tray outside.

Frankie shoved an arm across the door frame to block her. The tubes clanked as she came to a sudden halt. "Hold up, whatchya got there?"

She steadied the Scarlet tray. Frankie plucked out two of the Scarlet tubes.

"Mitch won't mind if we take a couple of samples, ya know?"

He unscrewed the top off one and downed half of it in one gulp. Billie ducked under his arm to get out onto the porch. She didn't know much about the drug, but she'd heard mentions of administering by eye-dropper, so she was pretty sure Frankie had just taken way too much.

Gil carried the duffle bag outside, but dropped it on the ground when he saw the vial Frankie held out to him. "Oh shit, is that Scarlet?" he said. "I've been wanting to try that."

Billie hurriedly opened the truck's back door and placed the tray of remaining tubes on the floor of the backseat. She picked up the abandoned bag and placed it on top of the tray, both to block the tray from sight and to hold the vials in place. Didn't Mitch have a secret compartment, a smuggler's hold somewhere in the truck? Probably, but her hands were shaking too much to search. She felt her skin ripple and she paused, closed her eyes, took a deep breath. She couldn't shift, not right now, not in front of Frankie and Gil, not without a set of clothes to replace the ones she'd likely tear if she didn't get them off in time. But oh, she wanted to. Shed this body and all its human troubles and race out into the comfort of the forest. She took another breath to quell the instinct, and when she was sure she could keep her skin, she opened her eyes again.

Billie turned around to see the two men romping around the driveway like hyper apes. Frankie's face was flushed, looking like he'd just held his breath for far too long. Gil pulled his shirt off, revealing a chest and back covered in wiry black hair, making him resemble a great ape even more. But beneath that hair, his skin had turned bright red, like he had an awful sunburn. Almost like Daniel's face had looked the night before.

Gil planted his foot on the tree trunk and managed a nearly supernatural flip, landing unsteadily. He wobbled a few steps, then crashed to the gravel. He stood up, tried the flip again, but his foot slipped and one broad shoulder collided with the tree. The trunk cracked dangerously, and Billie stepped back in alarm. He stumbled and collapsed on his stomach. Frankie laughed until he collapsed too.

No one really knew what Scarlet was made from, but it acted like part hallucinogen, part steroid, and Billie had heard of people lifting cars and doing other ridiculous feats while high. She'd always assumed it was hyperbole, like they just *felt* like they could do those things, or hallucinated that they did. But she was sober, and she'd just seen that weird flip with her own eyes.

Billie eased the truck's back door shut and peeled the gloves off. Unsure what to do with them, she stuffed the gloves into her jeans pocket, where they bulged awkwardly. Then she hesitated with her hand on the driver's side door. Frankie and Gil lay sprawled on the gravel driveway, while Toby's body lay just a few feet away, and for a moment Billie wondered if all three of them were dead. But Frankie and Gil's chests both heaved with labored breaths and the occasional maniacal giggle.

*Worst crime cleanup team ever*, Billie thought. "Do you... do you guys need me to stay until you sober up?"

Both of them sat suddenly upright and turned to look at her as though they'd just noticed she existed. They said nothing, but got to their feet and started stalking toward her, hungry looks on their faces. Billie slammed and locked the truck door, and peeled out of the driveway, leaving them behind in a spray of gravel.

Once she got back to the hotel, she stuffed the tubes into the bag anyway, in case she had to pass by any random patrons. The lobby was empty, though, and it was late enough that even the casino had cleared out except for one loud table in the corner and a few random hopefuls still pulling the slot machine levers in their eternal quest for that lucky combination. The scrape of her shoes across the carpet sounded loud to her ears. She tried to step softer, more catlike, but these human feet had no grace. Mitch's office door was propped open. She raised her fist to knock on the door frame, but he spotted her and clapped his hands together in a sharp burst that made her jump.

"There she is," he said.

He stood, rounded his desk and patted her on the back, guiding her to a chair. She fell into it with a thump. The tubes of Scarlet rattled in the bag as it landed roughly in her lap. Mitch kicked the doorstop up and let the door swing closed. She pulled the gloves out of her pocket and stuffed them into the duffle bag's side pouch, wondering if she might end up seeing them again in court someday, her skin cells extracted as evidence like in those crime shows Mitch loved so much.

"Really, a stand-out job," Mitch said. "How you holding up?"

"Little nervous," Billie said. That was an understatement. She'd been barely hanging on to her human form for the last hour, fighting the urge to shift and go hide in her cave until all of this had blown over. She normally had to concentrate in order to shift, but under stress like this she had to concentrate to *keep* from shifting. When she felt threatened in human form, her animal form tried to come out to protect her. Usually she could control it, but it had happened by accident a couple of times before. She'd had to pull the truck over several times on the way there just to keep herself together. Gently, she set the duffle bag on Mitch's desk.

"Well, that's to be expected. But you done good, kitty cat."

"Mitch, I didn't do it."

Mitch unzipped the bag and waved a dismissive hand at her. "Of course not, of course not."

"No, I'm serious. I didn't do it. He really was dead when I got there. I don't know who—what—killed him."

Mitch considered her for a moment. "Hmm. Okay." He pulled one of the rolls of money out of the duffle bag and tossed it at her. Billie caught it, just barely. "For a happy coincidence."

She clenched the roll in her fist and left without another word.

Downstairs, Billie remembered she didn't have the car. She glanced at the clock. It was three thirty a.m. She could either wait here for an hour and then call Caleb to ask for a ride on his way to the quarry, or she could walk home in the dark.

With whatever had killed Toby still prowling the night? With a roll of drug money too big to even fit in her pocket? It was only a mile and a half to the cabin, but still. Billie sighed and flopped down on a couch in the lobby to wait. She grabbed one of the complimentary notepads from a side table, with the Silver Coin logo and contact info printed across the top, and started folding the sheets into origami shapes to pass the time. She left the little paper animals littered all over the lobby.

"Do I even want to know?" Caleb asked when he picked her up, surely observing how disheveled and pale she looked, and eying the roll of money with suspicion.

"I'll tell you sometime," she said tiredly.

# TUESDAY

Billie slept surprisingly hard, but the memory of finding Toby Moran's body played itself on a loop through her dreams, the image warping into nonsense. She woke up to someone banging on the door. Again. The whole cabin rattled with each urgent knock. If her dad was back for another attempt at reconciliation, she couldn't deal with him. Not now. But when Billie glanced out the window and saw it was Mitch hammering his fist against the door frame instead, she unlocked the door. Before she could even open it, he pushed through, grabbed her arm and yanked her over toward the couch.

"Ow, Mitch, what the fuck?"

She stumbled against his stride and he yanked her arm harder, then pushed her so she fell onto the couch. He shoved a finger toward her face.

"There's only one thing I want you to tell me."

Billie swallowed. He towered over her. The hair on the back of her neck bristled and it was all she could do not to arch her back and hiss at him. If he grabbed her again, if he hit her, she would shift and give him the worst cat scratches he'd ever had.

"It has come to my attention this morning," Mitch started, sounding awkwardly formal, "that Gil Gorman and Frankie Cokes have both met an untimely and unexpected end." He dropped the finger and leaned in until he was close enough she could smell his sour breath. Billie flinched away from him, pressing herself deeper into the couch cushions. "*Why?*" He stretched the word out with an accusative lilt.

"What?" Billie said.

Mitch stood upright again, his hands clasped behind his back.

"Those were my two best men," he said through clenched teeth.

"Did they O.D.?" Billie asked. "They were messing with the Scarlet…"

"No!" Mitch barked. "They appear to have been ripped to shreds by some *animal*."

"I didn't do it! I didn't do any of it!"

Mitch just glowered at her.

Billie let out a long exhale and tried to loosen her grip on the couch pillow she held in her lap like some weak shield. "They were alive when I left them at Toby's. I didn't—I wouldn't—I *couldn't*—"

"Shh shh shh shh," Mitch said. He knelt down in front of the couch, taking her arms again. One hand was firm, the other stroked her arm like she was a pet. The unwanted touch grated on her already frayed nerves. She tried to pull away, but he held strong and there was nowhere she could go.

"I believe you," he said, voice softer now. "I didn't think my kitty cat would do something like that to me." She stared blankly into his chest.

"I swear," she said, nearly wheezing. It was hard to catch a full breath. She closed her eyes, willing herself to stay human. Her skin rippled. Mitch suddenly let go of her arms and she opened her eyes long enough to see him lean back, giving her a surprised look. She shut them again just as quickly, and kept them closed until she was sure that when she opened them, Mitch wouldn't see the golden irises and slip pupil of her cat eyes. She heard him get back to his feet with a grunt.

"But if it wasn't you," Mitch said, his voice sounding a little less confident, an edge of nervousness creeping in, "then I need you to do something. I need you to find out who did. Can you do that for me?"

"Um." Billie tentatively peeked her eyes open. Was he actually afraid of her? Feeling the shift start right beneath his hands seemed to have been enough to freak him out. He'd stepped back, putting the coffee table between them.

"Can you do that for me?" he repeated. And when she didn't respond, he said, "Let's say *yes*. Because I need this whole mess cleaned up before this weekend, okay?"

*Before the Fourth of July*, Billie knew he meant, when the town would be swarming with tourists, here to watch fireworks over the lake and spend money at his hotel. The biggest tourist draw of the year—the only thing that kept Juniper on the map as far as the rest of Colorado was concerned.

"And if I don't have an answer soon, I'll tell Caleb you did it." That signature confidence—or arrogance, rather—was back in his voice now. He'd figured out how to tilt the power back to himself now, or at least he thought he had.

All the air went out of Billie's lungs. "He won't—he won't believe you."

"No? He knows what you are. He knows you have to lie just to exist."

"He won't," she whispered, but she wasn't as sure as she wanted to be. Caleb and Mitch may have had their battles, but Mitch *was* his father, after all. Would Caleb side with him? Would he believe she was a monster?

"Or," Mitch said, "maybe I'll just have to tell the whole town about your special abilities. Good timing to out you, actually, with your father back in town now to confirm all those rumors about what really happened to your mother." Billie started to say something but he cut her off. "Oh yes, I know he's back. Nothing happens in this town that I don't hear about."

"Except who killed your boys," Billie said, and immediately regretted it.

"*Nothing*. You're going to find out who or what took out Frankie, Gil, and Toby, or we will hunt you out of town. You have until Friday." He slammed the door behind him, and the whole cabin rattled with the force.

After Mitch left, and after the buzz of anxiety softened enough that she could think again, Billie peeked out the front window and saw both a police car and a news van parked on the main street of a town that normally had neither. She snapped the blinds shut and went to find Caleb's computer, plugged it in, and searched. The news video showed up right at the top of the search engine.

A woman in a red dress jacket stood in the forest holding a microphone. Police tape crisscrossed between trees behind her. Billie recognized Toby's driveway and the side of his house in the background.

"An early morning hike in Clear Creek County became a nightmare when two hikers lost their way on a trail and discovered a grisly scene."

The footage flipped to one of the hikers, an out-of-towner in REI gear and sunglasses. "It was like something out of a horror movie. I still can't even believe it." Billie squinted at the man for a moment before she realized he was the same one who had been wearing the Broncos shirt at the ghost tour, half of the couple that Robyn was taking out to look at houses. "My wife and I saw the house," he was saying, "and realized we'd gotten off the trail somehow, figured we'd go up to the road to find our way back. Then we saw the bodies."

"Three men are confirmed dead in what appears to be an attack by a large animal," the reporter continued, "though local authorities have been unable to ascertain whether the attacker was a mountain lion, a bear, or something else."

Whatever had killed Toby must have come back while Frankie and Gil were stumbling around high on Scarlet. Could even have been lurking in the trees while she was there, Billie realized.

The screen zoomed out to show a map of the area, a red flag marking the attack site, several more noteworthy Colorado towns highlighted to orient viewers to the location of their obscure town. The reporter said, "The bodies were found at a home just outside the town of Juniper, Colorado around seven o'clock this morning." A quick shot of Toby's porch, then an establishing shot of a vacant Miners Avenue. Billie flinched to see her own porch peeking out behind the row of shops. It felt like a strange invasion of privacy to know this had been filmed while she slept. "Meanwhile, residents of this small town are left shaken, and worry that the attacks may not be an isolated event."

They had interviewed three Juniper residents: Randall Briggs, an old mountain man with the beard and flannel shirt to play the part, who declared, "If there's a killer lion out there, someone needs to take it out. We're not waiting for animal control to come pussy footing up here with their tranqs,"; Robyn Applebaum, in full makeup and styled hair as though she'd planned to be interviewed first thing this morning, who said, "I just can't *believe* something like this could happen to our sleepy little town. I've always felt so safe here before! I just hope whatever did this, they catch it soon so it doesn't interfere with our absolutely amazing Fourth of July festival,"; and Nick Musgrave, locally known as "Mouse," owner of Juniper's marijuana dispensary, who stared wide-eyed into the camera and said, "It was Bigfoot. I been telling people for years that he's out there, and now, I guess he's *pissed*."

Billie rolled her eyes. Real quality cross-section of the community they captured there.

"The victims have been identified as Franklin Cokes, Tobias Moran, and Gilbert Gorman, all residents of Juniper. More on this story as it develops."

The screen showed what looked like driver's license photos of Frankie and Gil, only slightly less morose than mugshots would have been, and a blurry selfie of Toby, taken from his Facebook profile and cropped so as not to show the middle finger he'd been giving the camera.

The reporter signed off and the video switched to something about a suspected religious cult in Boulder that had been recruiting college students. Billie shut the laptop and pushed it away from her. She plunked elbows onto the table and rubbed her hands vigorously across her face. Mitch had threatened to throw her under the bus as a scapegoat if she didn't find the killer. The Juniper locals would probably believe him, especially if he had some evidence to show them, which he probably did. Had he added some surveillance cameras in the parking garage where she had shifted to chase Daniel the other night? That's all it would take for them to string her up. The police wouldn't buy it any more than Mouse's Bigfoot theory, but Randall was sure to track down some innocent bear they could all blame. And, *oh no, look, the killer bear just happened to get one more victim before they caught it, just some bartender at the Silver Coin, how sad.* The news would move on to the next drug bust or political scandal in no time. The town would be rid of a witch, the tourists would be safe, and everyone would be happy. Until whatever had actually killed the three men struck again.

Well, she couldn't very well figure anything out sitting in her cabin worrying about it. She glanced out the front window. The car was there, which meant Caleb must have carpooled with his friend Brock to work today, as he often did. She wished he was here right now, so she could tell him everything that had happened, explain it all before Mitch tried to turn him against her. He wouldn't believe she'd killed those men, would he? She wasn't as sure as she wanted to be about that.

She changed out of her pajamas into jeans and a tank top, and drove out to Toby's house. A single police car guarded it, and police tape crisscrossed the driveway. A policewoman aggressively waved her on when Billie slowed the car. Of course it was still closed down. What did Mitch think she could find that the police couldn't, anyway? In bobcat form, she might be able to detect scent signatures, follow trails that humans couldn't identify. But the official story was that the men had been killed by a large animal, and while "bobcat" was probably not first on the list of suspects, it might get there if anyone saw her skulking around the property.

Billie turned the car around in someone else's driveway, and two large black dogs raced up to chase her car down the street, barking and snapping at her tires. *A dog could work*, she thought absently. She was out of practice trying any other forms, didn't know if she could even manage it anymore.

Her dad had brought home a dog once, a big scruffy stray that he had found wandering out by the river. He'd tied it up in the backyard, and Billie's mother had thrown a fit. Billie had been, what, seven? Eight? She was on the living room floor fitting together a puzzle when they started fighting.

"We can't have a dog in this house," Billie's mom said.

"Why not? He'll keep the coyotes away. He won't hurt nobody."

"I'm just not a dog person!" she said exasperatedly.

"So? He'll live outside. Billie can feed him, isn't that right?" Her dad looked down and gave Billie a wink. Billie glanced uneasily at her mom and then back down to her puzzle. He often tried to pull her into their fights, to get her to side with him. Unless it was something minor like "which ice cream flavor should we get," Billie usually just kept her mouth shut.

"You didn't even *ask* me," Billie's mom said.

"I don't *need* to ask you anything, I'm the man of this house..."

As the fight continued, Billie shoved her puzzle pieces back toward her pile of toys and crept through the kitchen to the back door, as she often did when they were fighting, which was becoming more frequent. They didn't notice she was gone. Usually, she would wait out their fights on the back porch. From there, the voices were still angry vibrations rattling the walls, but she couldn't understand most of the words. But today, as soon as she clicked the porch door shut behind her, the dog stood up to greet her. He walked to the end of the rope that tied him to a tree, and wagged a matted, scruffy tail. She approached cautiously, holding a hand out to the dog. He strained toward her, gave her hand three quick, audible sniffs, then a slobbery lick. Billie giggled.

"You need a bath." The dog's fur was matted and caked with dried mud. Billie uncoiled the garden hose, stomping out the kinks, and turned it on. The dog practically flipped over itself trying to get away from the sudden spray, but Billie chased it down, and the dog snapped at the stream of water as its fur got soaked. Then the back door slammed open and Billie turned in surprise to see her dad clomping down the porch stairs. The look on his face was pure rage. Billie dropped the hose. He crossed the yard to her in a few long strides and grabbed her arm, rougher than he'd ever grabbed her before, all the tenderness and playfulness she was used to from him gone. The wet dog cowered behind the tree it was tied to. Billie had never truly felt scared of her dad before, but now her skin rippled the way it did just before a shift, and she knew if he kept yanking her toward the house, the fear would drive her into a shift, even though she'd promised her mom never to shift in front of her dad. He let go of her arm, suddenly, giving her a peculiar look.

He pointed toward the house. "Inside."

Billie ran. She told her mom that he had grabbed her arm, and that led to another fight, though not until after he came back from wherever he'd taken the dog. She never knew what had become of the dog, and realized much later that she probably didn't *want* to know.

Back on Miners Avenue, Billie parked the car in front of her cabin, but instead of going inside, she opened the gate to the backyard, then squeezed through a gap in the fence. The building next door was an old livery stable, long abandoned. The back door hung off its hinges, and she moved it aside just enough to step through. She clapped a couple of times to scare out any new inhabitants, human or animal, but it only made the dust swirl in the few sunbeams that managed to break through the boarded-up windows. Billie stripped off her clothes, laying them on top of the others she'd left there a few days before.

"I'm just not a dog person," Billie whispered, remembering her mother's shouted words, but she gave it a try anyway, attempting to fold and shape her body into something more canine than feline.

It took a couple of tries, but finally Billie thought she had something. She looked down at paws that were narrower than normal, short-furred legs that were longer and skinner than the fluffy spotted legs of a bobcat. There was a dusty mirror leaning against one wall of the abandoned building, so she trotted over there to see what she'd become. Even moving that small distance was awkward; this body felt lanky and clumsy, and she really had to think about how to move each leg. She laughed when she looked in the mirror, though it came out as a sharp bark. She'd managed a dog form, alright, but it was the weirdest-looking mutt she'd ever seen, almost like a real-life version of a six-year-old's drawing of a dog. The ears were different sizes, the eyes different colors, and her fur was still spotted in the same bobcat pattern, making her look almost like a hyena. If anyone saw her skulking around the crime scene like this, they'd definitely decide she was a Chupacabra. Not exactly a good cover, under the circumstances.

She unfolded back to human form, thought about the dog her dad had brought home, and tried again. This time, she ended up something like a cross between an Irish Wolfhound and a Catahoula, with short, floppy ears, a long jowly snout, and a thin tail twice as long as what she had as a bobcat. Her eyes were still mismatched, one blue and one brown, and her wiry fur was lightly spotted. It seemed no matter what form she took, Billie was stuck with the freckles that blotched her human face. This was still an odd-looking dog, but a friendly one, at least. Someone might assume this animal was the one responsible for digging the moldy nachos out of their trashcan, but they wouldn't suspect it was capable of slaughtering three grown men.

Billie gave a sniff, and was glad to find that her senses were just as sharp as in cat form. Maybe more, even. She could smell the racoon that was nested on the second floor of the building, could tell that it was about to give birth to a litter any day now. She could identify the scent signature that she knew as Caleb's faintly drifting over from next door, faded but ever-present. She could tell that the bar down the street had burned a hamburger in the kitchen. She plodded around the room for a moment, testing to see if she could maintain this form. It was uncomfortable, but tolerable. She squeezed out of the back door, jumped the fence, and headed toward Toby's.

It was a long way to go, and navigating the forest as a dog was cumbersome. Her paws struck the earth loudly, the unfamiliar body awkward and lacking all the grace and surefootedness she had as a cat. She couldn't see as well, and the information she got through the dog's whiskers was so light they were practically useless. But she plodded on, nose to the ground to search for any scents out of the ordinary. She overshot Toby's house by a quarter mile on purpose, keeping out of sight among the trees, then padded across the road and approached from the side, down a steep slope and across a rocky wash that funneled into a waterfall when it rained.

Behind the house, Billie tasted the air, trying to parse out the scents. There were a lot of them: blood and fear still present beneath the layers of the dozens of people who had been to the crime scene this morning. Through scents, she could often identify age, sex, and sometimes diet or health issues, but with so many competing layers here, nothing very useful was coming through. Except, she did note, all the scent signatures she could identify were distinctly human. No mountain lion, no bear. Had the animal's scent simply dissipated in the wind, or been overwritten by the presence of so many people?

Or had there been no animal, after all?

As she searched, she took care to step on pine needles or aspen leaves as often as possible to avoid leaving pawprints in the soil. The only animal prints near the scene belonged to deer or rabbit. The perimeter of the crime scene had been taped off, with flags marking—she assumed—where the bodies had been found. Ribbons around two trees marked blood stains, and they'd missed a third splash across the leaves of a bush. The police officer she'd seen earlier was nowhere in sight, though the police car was still there, so she ventured closer to the driveway, searching for scents where the bodies had lain. Here was the blood, and the Scarlet—almost indistinguishable from blood, a slight grape-like scent mixed with the tangy copper—and the lingering stench of car exhaust. Male scent trails, full of adrenaline and testosterone. Nothing that told her anything she didn't already know.

She was just about to give up when she found one thing just outside of the orange tape, inexplicable and out of place. Near the edge of the driveway was a footprint.

A bare, human footprint.

Just one, pointed away from the scene of the attack. Billie stared at the print for a long moment, trying to make sense of it. Then she slowly dipped her head toward the print and tried to parse the extremely faint scent signature. Male, adult, malnourished—someone suffering from the kind of hunger that meant your own muscles were beginning to be metabolized. And something that might have been alcohol—or maybe just more of the Scarlet? This scent could have been Toby's. He'd been very dead by the time Frankie and Gil got there. Billie had seen him herself. And all three bodies had been recovered by the police, so it was unlikely that he'd somehow risen from the dead, attacked Frankie and Gil, and run off into the woods. If something like that had happened, the news report probably would have been very different this morning.

Which left Billie with one, very uncomfortable, conclusion.

There might be another shapeshifter in Juniper.

Caleb sped down Miners Avenue and turned onto the winding mountain road out of town a little too fast.

"Don't you wreck my car, dawg," Brock said from the passenger seat. He clutched at the overhead handhold, grimacing. Caleb looked down at the First-Aid Kit bandages around Brock's leg. He'd already bled all the way through them.

"Hey, you keep telling me how to drive, I'll throw your limping ass in the trunk," Caleb said.

Brock smirked, but the expression faded into a wince. Caleb pushed the gas a little bit more.

The rockslide had happened just after lunch break, and Brock had been the only one in the quarry unlucky enough to get caught in it. Caleb and two others had hefted the boulder off of his leg. It would have taken an hour, at least, for an ambulance to make it up to Juniper, so as soon as they'd decided this was worse than the tiny local clinic could handle, Caleb had volunteered to drive him down to the closest hospital. It was forty miles away, practically to Breckenridge.

"You're just lucky I wasn't driving my own car today," Caleb said, mostly just to keep Brock's attention. "Better you bleed all over your own junk heap."

Brock didn't respond.

"Hey, man," Caleb said. "You stay awake, we've still got a long way to go."

Though he wanted to speed up again, Caleb did slow down as they approached the hairpin turn just past the Silver Coin. He'd been in one car wreck there already, and had no desire to repeat the crash, especially with an already-injured passenger.

It had happened the summer before he left for college. He'd ridden to a house party with some friends, including his new girlfriend, who had been reluctant to go that far out of town, though she wouldn't tell him why. His dad had apparently gotten wind of the party, and came banging on the door, threatening arrest and lawsuits and beatings and whatever else he thought might scare Caleb and his friends. Caleb and Billie left with him, and he continued to yell on the way back to the Silver Coin, which was "home" back then, though Caleb had never felt like a third floor hotel room where he wasn't allowed to hang anything on the walls and could hear tourists fucking next door really deserved the label "home." His dad was probably driving a little too fast, not paying enough attention to the tight turns of the mountain road, especially on the hairpin turn, where it was so easy to drift out of your own lane if you weren't going the recommended snail speed. The crash had sent the truck sliding sideways and pinned them precariously against the guard rail—a lucky thing it was there, since on the other side was a drop of at least fifty feet until the closest treetops, further to hit the steep slope of ground.

But the most shocking thing about the experience had been turning to the back seat to check on his girlfriend and seeing not the freckled girl in jeans and a ponytail he'd gone to the party with, but a large bobcat sitting where she had been, a purple tank top stretched absurdly across its fur. The creature had stared back at him with seemingly equal surprise. His dad had muttered, "What the hell?" as he looked into the rear-view mirror, and then the person from the other car shined a flashlight through the window to ask if they were okay. When Caleb had looked again, Billie was in the back seat where the cat had been, tugging at her clothes and giving him an embarrassed scowl.

As Caleb passed the spot where his dad's truck had crashed, Brock groaned, and put his hand to his head again, smearing blood across his forehead.

"We're almost there, man," Caleb lied as they cleared the hairpin turn. He sped as fast as he dared down the mountain roads toward the hospital.

After Brock was admitted and rolled away on an emergency room stretcher, Caleb stood outside in the hospital courtyard. Spots of Brock's blood speckled his dirt-stained jeans. He took a long breath to try to still the shaking of his hands, and then called Tara, Brock's wife.

She was hysterical. Caleb held the phone away from his ear as she screamed, and had to yell over her to tell her Brock was probably going to be fine, and Caleb would be back with the car later that evening. He couldn't remember for sure if they were a one-car couple like he and Billie, but either way, he encouraged her to just wait, saying he might even be able to bring Brock home that night. Tara cried and yelled some more, and eventually he just hung up on her. *Yeesh.* It was like she'd never had to deal with a crisis before.

He passed the phone back and forth between his hands a few times, savoring the relative silence of the courtyard. A few pigeons warbled from a window ledge. Traffic hummed from the road on the other side of the building. The automatic glass doors whooshed as someone else walked outside. All very different from the too-familiar sounds of Juniper: bulldozers and crumbling rock, wind through the trees, the creak of boots on ancient wooden stairs.

He called Billie, and she… wasn't there. No surprise. She never answered his calls. Took forever to return his texts. She didn't have a smartphone, and said texting was cumbersome on her old-fashioned flip phone. That was only part of it, though, and they both knew it. He didn't blame her, although sometimes he wanted to. He blamed his dad, for keeping her on a tight leash in order to punish him. God, how he wanted out of that town.

While they'd waited on the tow truck to come retrieve Mitch's truck from the crash at the hairpin turn, Mitch had confronted Billie about what he'd seen in the back seat. If he hadn't, Caleb probably would have chalked it up to having too many Everclear shots, some weird interplay of the shadows and adrenaline with his liquor-soaked mind. But his dad had seen the girl become a cat too, and he wouldn't stop pestering her until she finally whispered, "I'm a shapeshifter. My mom was too. I don't know anyone else who can do it, but it happens sometimes when I'm scared."

"Witchcraft," his dad had said.

"*No*," Billie said with unexpected force, and Caleb recalled the rumors he'd heard about her when he first moved here, the way some of his friends had warned him to stay away from her when she started working at the Silver Coin.

"Please don't tell anyone," she pleaded. Her hands were shaking, and Caleb swore her eyes had more of a yellow tinge than normal.

"We won't tell anyone," Caleb said, and his dad had grunted something that might have been agreement.

After he found out Billie's secret, Caleb had felt closer to her, protective of her, fascinated by her. Every break when the dorms closed and forced him back up to Juniper, he fell in love with Billie all over again. But every time he had to stay in that reconstructed monstrosity of a tourist trap his dad called a hotel, the relationship with his dad grew more and more strained, as he lied to him about the classes he was taking, refused to engage in conversations about what was going to come next. Caleb had had a plan to leave that place for good once he graduated, but Billie wouldn't come with him. *Couldn't*, or so she said. And he couldn't leave her. So here they were, trapped in his dad's malicious web.

And here he was, waiting to find out if his friend was going to lose a leg, keenly aware that it could just as easily have been himself under the rockslide. That if it *had* been him, and he'd needed Billie to drive him to the hospital, she wouldn't have been able to do it. Fortunately, a nurse came out to the courtyard before he got too far into that spiral of thoughts, and told him he could see Brock now.

They'd put him in a double room, with a drooling old man in the bed next to him, a flimsy curtain splitting the room. A nurse adjusted an IV bag beside his bed. Brock's leg was propped up on a pillow, wrapped in a cast.

"Hey, asshole," Caleb said by way of friendly greeting, slapping Brock's arm softly with the back of his hand. "I was looking forward to making fun of your peg leg, but looks like you get to keep it."

Brock's head rolled toward him and he lifted a middle finger in response. *Yeah, he's alright,* Caleb thought.

"The leg has been set and the wound is bandaged, but he lost a lot of blood, so we're going to keep him overnight," the nurse explained.

After the nurse left, Caleb plopped himself into the visitor's chair. The curtain blocked the other patient's bed, but Caleb could still hear them snoring.

"Did you see it?" Brock said.

"Did I see what?"

"At the top of the hill."

"The rockslide? Nah, it happened so fast."

Brock shook his head, then winced at the movement. "No, dawg. There was someone up there."

"Whole crew was down below. It was just an accident, man."

"No," Brock whispered, the word an urgent hiss. "Caleb, listen. It wasn't an accident."

The fact that Brock used his real name made Caleb move a little closer, listen with a little more attention.

"What do you mean?"

"I saw… there was a face. Like a man, but like an animal too."

"What?"

"It—he—it pushed the boulder, dawg."

"You saw someone push the boulder that started the rockslide. For real?"

"It was like, stalking me. Looked all panicked that I'd noticed it, and pushed the boulder toward me."

"I'll tell the foreman. You think it was one of the bastards who squats in those abandoned cabins? I'll burn those fucking places down."

"It wasn't a man. At least, not fully. It was like a… lobster. But with a man's face."

"A lobster man?" Caleb couldn't help but laugh. "In the forest?"

"Whatever, dawg," Brock said, and rolled his head away.

Caleb knew because of Billie that science didn't know everything. Or else didn't admit everything it knew, for whatever messed up reasons. But chances were that Brock was high on hospital painkillers, chemicals warping his memories. Trauma demanded he blame someone, find some reason behind what had happened to him.

"It was—" Brock started again, but then the doctor came in with a clipboard and Brock stopped talking.

She squinted at Caleb. "Are you family?"

"Just a friend. I drove him here."

"Hmm," the doctor said, sounding almost disapproving. Then she turned to Brock. "Mr. Dwyer. How long have you been taking Scarlet?"

"What?" Brock said. "I haven't—"

She turned the clipboard toward him. "Tox-screen shows evidence of alcohol, marijuana, and Scarlet in your bloodstream. And not in small amounts."

"Shit," Brock said. "You going to turn me in?"

"Technically, none of those are illegal substances. But they all impair your judgment, the Scarlet in particular. So, once again, how long have you been taking Scarlet?"

"I only tried it a couple of times," Brock admitted after a moment.

Caleb groaned. It was no wonder he was talking about forest lobsters if he was taking Scarlet. Worst part was, this might make his workers comp case harder to defend and he'd be stuck with a bum leg and unpayable medical bills.

"Were you high when the accident occurred?"

"No."

The scathing glare the doctor gave Brock reminded Caleb of his middle school English teacher, and under normal circumstances he'd have enjoyed watching his friend squirm under that gaze.

"Really!" Brock nearly squeaked.

Caleb's phone buzzed. Billie, finally. He squeezed past the doctor while she continued to grill Brock on his history with the drug. Caleb sent one sympathetic glance back toward Brock.

In the hallway, Caleb called Billie back and put a finger to his ear to block out the hospital sounds.

"What? No, it wasn't an animal attack," he told Billie. "Brock just had an accident at work."

Billie sniffed at the footprint, trying to discern which direction the scent trail led. She flinched at a sudden clap, and then the police officer was there, yelling at her to get away. At least her assessment of using a dog form had been correct; she wasn't perceived as a threat. She darted into the forest, following the faint scent trail in a straight line toward Juniper Ridge, a sheer cliff that overlooked the south side of town, but then she lost it as she intersected a hiking trail, where too many overlapping scents competed.

Since her powers were limited by her territory, then if there was another shapeshifter in town now, it must be someone local. But how could she not know who it was? How could she have lived so close to someone with her same ability and not discovered them? Wouldn't they have reached out to her after what happened to her mother?

Her spine rippled. *Strange*, she thought, but she *had* been shifted for several hours now, and this unfamiliar shape took a lot of effort. Better head to the cave, in any case. She was on the primary trail that looped around the entire perimeter of Juniper. If she followed it for about a mile, there would be a fork that led down to the lake behind the Silver Coin Hotel. Her cave was inside a hidden rocky outcropping near there. She plodded along the trail as quickly as she could, ready to dart into the trees at the first sign of people, but no one seemed to be out on the trails today.

When she was close enough that she could see the tumble of boulders that obscured her cave, her body heaved with a dizzy swirl of nausea. She stopped in her tracks, fighting to keep her human form from bursting out of the dog form. It didn't work. Her body unfolded, released like a taut spring finally let go. She stood upright and looked around. At least no one had been around to see that, as far as she could tell. *Strike two*, she thought. Two times now that she'd shifted in an indiscreet location where someone might have been able to see her. She crossed arms over her breasts and climbed up to the cave as quickly as she could. Rocks and pine needles stabbed at her toes. The forest floor was far less kind to bare human feet than it was to animal paws.

Twice in the past, she had shifted into bobcat form without intending to, both times when she'd been afraid for her life. Once had been when she was a very young child and had fallen out of a tree while climbing with a friend. Because they were three years old, no one taken it seriously when the friend told her parents about Billie turning into a cat, and the incident had been quickly forgotten by all. The other had been in a car wreck with Caleb and Mitch. Mitch had demanded she explain what he'd seen, and she'd eventually decided that telling him was safer than denying it. The secret had been what killed her mother, after all. Some days she regretted that choice more than others. When Mitch had given her the first spying task, she'd thought her abilities had made her more valuable to him. Eventually she realized it just gave him more leverage over her.

But she'd never lost her animal form on accident before.

Maybe Toby's house was too far away from her territory. Had she spread her powers too thin by being out there for so long? Her mother had never drawn the exact boundaries for her, and Billie had never been brave enough to test them. As she'd grown up, she'd become less and less willing to risk losing this one thing that made her special.

She ducked into her cave, lit the lantern, and pulled on one of the sets of clothes she had stashed in there, along with one of the cheap pairs of boots that looked the same as most of her others.

She downed the bottle of water she kept in the cave, but her stash of food had run out, and hunger was making her head swirl. It was closer to go to the Silver Coin, although that meant she'd likely be stuck there for the rest of the day. Just outside the cave, where she could get reception, she flipped opened her phone and paused when she saw a text from Caleb.

*Taking Brock to hospital.*

Billie called him immediately. It went to voicemail, and a surge of panic rose in her gut. She took off running toward home, and slowed when the phone vibrated with his return call.

Caleb said he was at the hospital in Frisco and would fill her in on all the details later, but she did manage to get enough information out of him to learn that his co-worker Brock had been injured by a rockslide at the quarry, and did not appear to have been attacked by an animal.

"Just a bad day all around," she said before they hung up. She walked the whole way back to the cabin, and she was so hungry by the time she got there that she ate the entire leftover meatloaf that was supposed to have been their dinner that evening.

Billie sat on the couch, recovering from heartburn, and made a list of locals who could maybe, possibly, be shapeshifters. Mouse, maybe? He could be using his Bigfoot obsession to distract people. She'd never known *why*, exactly, he had been nicknamed "Mouse." Or Heather, the owner of the Enchanted Mountain Metaphysical Shop downtown? But no, a job like that wouldn't be a good front. Mr.

Martin, the high school math teacher—but she only thought that because he was hairy as a bear already. What about—

A gunshot outside cracked the air. Billie jumped and nearly dropped her pen.

"What now?" she groaned, and slammed the Silver Coin notepad and pen onto the coffee table. She pulled back the curtain to see a crowd clogging Miners Avenue. Tentatively, she opened the front door and stepped outside.

People filled the street, and for a moment Billie was afraid she'd somehow slept for four days and woken up in the middle of the Fourth of July festivities. That was the only time Juniper was ever this crowded. A Subaru honked and tried unsuccessfully to navigate through the sea of bodies. She looked around for the news van, but if it was still in town, she couldn't spot it. Someone was talking through a megaphone, the words unintelligible from that far away.

Billie pressed her way through the crowd until she could see who held the megaphone. It was Randall Briggs, standing in the center of the gazebo on the far end of Miners Avenue. Two signs hung from the sides of the gazebo: poster board pictures of an angry mountain lion inside a circle, crossed out with a slash, the text below proclaiming, "Protect our Community."

"Three men," Randall was saying as Billie came into earshot. "Grown men, and long-time residents of this community, not soft city tourists who think the mountains are their playground. If *they're* not safe, do you really think your children are safe? We've got a man-killer running loose around here, and I say it's high time we do something about it."

The crowd cheered, clapped, egged him on. Billie groaned again. Pitchforks and torches were imminent.

"Now," Randall said, "official 'hunting season' for mountain lions isn't until November. So we can wait around, do the paperwork, get the license, and roll the dice about how many of our neighbors get picked off in the next four months. Or we say to hell with all that bureaucratic bullshit and do something about this problem ourselves, *right now.*"

Isolated yells of agreement sparked up from the crowd. Randall jabbed his finger toward the floor of the gazebo to punctuate his next point.

"We don't need no damn forestry officials or wildlife activists telling us what we can and can't do to protect ourselves. We take care of our own up here. We can't afford to wait until hunting season. Not when *we're* the ones being hunted."

Choruses of "That's right" and whistles of approval echoed through the crowd like a Pentecostal church congregation. Randall started pacing around the gazebo.

"But I did bring in one outsider," he said. "Cousin of mine. Called him this morning as soon as I heard."

He waved to someone in the crowd and a large man joined him, standing on the gazebo steps with thumbs through belt loops.

"This here's my cousin Wallace. He's a professional big game hunter. Runs hunting tours out of Glenwood Springs through Big-Game-Colorado-dot-com. Did I get that right?" Wallace nodded. "See, told you I'd remember. Anyway, you have any questions about hunting big cats, this is your man. Now I wanna keep this local. Don't go posting about it on the internets, or telling any of those lurking reporters what we're up to. But let's show them killer lions that they don't fuck with Juniper."

A bloodthirsty cry rose from the crowd. Randall lowered his megaphone and shook hands with Wallace.

"This is wrong." The whole crowd seemed to turn in unison toward the lone voice of dissent that finally broke through the chaos. "You don't even know it was a mountain lion. You can't just go wipe them all out."

Billie winced when she realized the voice belonged to her dad. He emerged from the crowd and climbed the gazebo steps. He said something more quietly directly to Randall, who listened stoic-faced for a moment, then raised the megaphone back up to his lips.

"Looks like we have some local opposition. From a man who shot his own damn wife. What's wrong, Keith, you advocate shooting women but not cats?"

The crowd booed and yelled. Billie's dad was saying something, but without the megaphone and beneath the roar of the crowd, none of his words reached anyone's ears.

"—might not be what you think it is," finally broke through.

Randall raised the megaphone. "Okay, he's got a fair point. He says maybe the killer wasn't a mountain lion. And you know what, he's right. We don't know for sure. Could have been a bear. Or, hell, it might have even been a person who arranged it to look like an animal. It sure would take a sicko to do something like that. Someone who had killed before." Billie noticed how thin her dad was, his shoulders hunched forward, ribs bowed in. Emaciated almost. *Male, adult, malnourished.* The information from the scent signature of the footprint certainly could have been his.

"Funny, isn't it?" Randall was saying, "How the one member of our community who has gone to prison for murder—"

"Manslaughter," he shouted. "The charge was manslaughter."

"—comes back just in time for a couple of other members of our community to suddenly drop dead. That is *quite* the coincidence, don't you think?"

Billie's dad looked like a deer caught in headlights. The crowd was shouting again, a mix of accusations and confusion.

"So which is it, man or beast?" Randall said. "Do we want to risk either one?"

Before Billie even realized she was doing it, she had pushed to the front of the crowd and inserted herself between the two of them.

"Stop this," she growled at Randall, who just looked at her with a bemused grin. "Go hunt your killer cat if it makes you feel powerful, but stop this. He didn't do it."

There was no point trying to get through the throng of people, so

Billie led her dad into the Enchanted Mountain Metaphysical Shop just to the right of the gazebo. He followed her past the displays of crystals and dreamcatchers. Billie lifted the flip-up counter beside the cash register, ignoring the protest of the high school student who worked there, went through the storage area and kicked open the back door. There was a dumpster out there, and some pipes and meters, and someone's bike propped against the wall. Randall's voice drifted over the buildings, saying something about how he knew it was a mountain lion because of the size of the claw marks and the strength needed to take down men like Frankie and Gil.

"Billie, baby doll—"

Billie rounded on her dad. This "baby doll" thing was even worse than Mitch's "kitty cat." Had he called her that when she was a child? Had it been endearing, comforting, back then? She couldn't even remember.

"Did you kill those men?"

"*No,*" he said fiercely. He put his hands on her arms, a firm but gentle grip. She stepped out of his reach, rubbing her hands across her arms to scrub away the residual discomfort of his touch.

"But you know who did," she guessed.

He seemed baffled. "No! I just don't want those assholes to go around shooting every lion in the county. I was afraid for you, Billie. You can't… while they're out there hunting, you need to, to, stay how you are."

He must assume she took the same shape as his late wife; he'd probably never even seen the little bobcat scratching her ear at the edge of the yard that night. Maybe he really was trying to protect her. Billie considered him. If he knew who the real killer was, it wouldn't make much sense to charge up there and object to Randall's red herring hunt. He could have done what Randall accused, but why? He didn't even know the men who had been killed. Maybe a favor for someone he met in prison? But even if he had, that didn't explain the footprint. So far, nothing did, except the inexplicable existence of another shifter.

"If you're not involved in this," she said, "then you should probably get back to wherever you're staying, before they lynch you in the streets for no reason." She started to walk away.

"Truck's broken down," he shouted after her.

Billie stopped, and without turning around, asked where he was staying. He named the area and she realized it was way up a long road, but on the side of town that wouldn't require trying to drive through the crowd like the Subaru that had been stuck earlier. She sighed.

"Come on," she said after a moment. She didn't even look back to see if he followed her along the river. Rounding the corner of the building across from her cabin, she could see that the mob was still focused on Randall, who appeared to be organizing teams and assigning them hunting territories to cover. This *would* make it practically impossible for her to shift, and dangerous to be out in the forest at all for the next couple of days. Maybe they would find whoever or whatever had killed the men, and she'd be off the hook. If it *was* another shapeshifter, though, they would surely have the sense to stay the hell out of the forest like she planned to.

She reached just inside the cabin door to grab the car keys that dangled from a peg on the wall, then sat in the driver's seat and waited for her dad to get in the passenger side. Once he did, she pulled a tight U-turn and drove away from the crowd.

"I know you're not glad to see me," he said after they'd been driving for a couple of minutes. "But I'm so glad to see you. Thirteen years, baby doll. You look—" He glanced away, and Billie knew he must have been about to say she looked like her mother. She didn't, though. She looked too much like him, and she'd remembered that every time she saw her own human face in a mirror, all these years.

The road curved and bumped uphill, following the river that flowed through town and eventually emptied into the lake behind the hotel. A few years ago, there had been bad flooding that had practically washed this road away and trapped the people who lived back here. But today the stream only burbled pleasantly along.

"This one?" she pointed to a turnoff and he nodded.

She drove up the dirt road, which twisted in switchbacks. There were a few houses up here, but mostly the road she ended up on existed to get to the fire tower at the top, a brick lookout that was only sometimes occupied by a forestry service member. If he was staying up here, it meant he was probably squatting in an old homestead or an illegal shack with no electricity or running water. Some people chose that lifestyle, but he probably did it because there was no way he could pay the inflated local prices that people like Robyn and Mitch had caused with their tourism draws. She tried not to feel sorry for him, but a tinge of sympathy did creep in.

"How long have you been up here?" she asked.

"Just a couple of weeks," he said. "I didn't come back here right away when they… when I got out. I worked for a few months in Denver. Had some money saved. But everything seemed pointless, without her, without you. I started sleeping in the mountains up by Boulder, just expecting to be attacked by a mountain lion. It seemed like the only logical path my life could follow at that point. I saw one, twice. The same one, I think. But she never attacked, she just slunk by."

He trailed off. Billie drove in silence. He stared at the floor and wrung his hands.

"I went to Durango for a while," he started again, but Billie wasn't interested in letting him talk. They were already at the lookout, and she parked the car and stepped outside.

There was no one at the fire tower today. It had been a quiet summer: plenty of rain and no fires except for one a good deal to the north, almost at the Wyoming border. The ground around the lookout was littered with cigarette butts and a fair amount of broken glass, some of it still in jagged shards, some of it so crushed that it blended in with the pebbles, bits of green or black shining among the quartz and granite. The wind was colder up here, biting at Billie's ears despite the summer sun. She could see the town of Juniper below, roofs peeking out between trees, roads through the forest like termite trails through a log. A few mountains over, the trees were dead from pine beetle infestation, brown and brittle, like lines of grave markers left in tribute to their former lives.

Her dad's boots crunched on the gravel behind her.

"Wherever it is you live, you can walk from here," she said. She was sure this was pretty much the edge of her territory. She wasn't going to leave it for him.

"Just promise me you won't—while those guys are hunting—that you won't—"

"Say it," she said. "Acknowledge what I am. No one else is here. Just say it."

He hesitated a long moment. "Promise me you won't shapeshift."

She stared straight ahead at the landscape. "You don't get to ask me for things like promises. I owe you *nothing*."

He leaned against the stone wall of the lookout. "If there was anything I could do to bring your mama back, I would do it. I wish so hard that I could do it. But I'm here now, and I hope that someday you'll let me back into your life."

Billie wiped away a tear that she hadn't realized had leaked out. She shook her head, pushed away from the lookout wall.

"The only reason I want to hear from you right now is if you learn anything about who or what killed Frankie, Gil, and Toby, okay?"

She drove off and left him at the lookout, swearing she could still feel his eyes watching her the whole drive back to town.

Billie had been home about two minutes when she got a call from Caleb asking her to come pick him up from Brock's house. Back into the car again. The crowd from earlier had cleared out, but the sign calling for the slaughter of killer mountain lions still hung in the gazebo. Billie shook her head as she drove past it. She was no closer to having an answer for Mitch yet, and the hunters wouldn't stop until they had some kind of trophy, whether it was the real killer or not.

Brock lived along one of the streets that started in town and snaked up into the forest along Shadow Ridge. While Toby's driveway had been a steep downhill, Brock's went uphill, and it was uneven and bumpy with tire ruts.

Caleb sat on the porch with Tara, Brock's wife. Billie didn't know much about her, only that she'd been a ski bum in Breckenridge and that she and Brock had been married less than a year. Both were in their mid-thirties, around ten years older than she and Caleb. Brock's car was parked in the driveway, and two other vehicles were parked in an open garage, one of them missing tires and a hood. Billie kept the car running and stepped out, leaning over the doorframe. Caleb told Tara, "Let me know when they let him out, 'kay?"

Tara nodded, then waved vigorously to Billie. Her makeup was smeared and her face was red from crying. Billie lifted a hand to wave back.

"Are you sure we should leave her alone like this?" Billie asked once Caleb slid into the passenger seat.

"She's going over to the hospital soon."

Billie navigated back down the rough driveway.

"Hell of a day," Caleb said once they were on the main road.

"Yeah, here too," Billie said. "What happened with Brock?"

Caleb told her about the rock slide at the quarry, and how Brock had gotten his leg caught under a large boulder.

"He was trying to tell me that some creature pushed the rocks down."

Billie frowned. "Did anyone else see what he was talking about?"

"No! It was just the shock talking. Actually, it may have been more than that. Guess what the doctor found in his system once we got him there? *Scarlet*. It's no wonder he was seeing things if he's coming to work high on *that* shit."

That got Billie's attention. If Brock was taking Scarlet, he'd likely gotten it from Toby. Maybe he knew something. Anything, really, might give her a better clue than what she already had.

"When will they let him out of the hospital?"

"Tomorrow, probably. Tara said something about a cougar attack here?"

Billie filled him in on what had been happening. She decided to skip the part about Mitch asking her to take out Toby, and started at finding the body. She skipped the part about Randall's lion hunt, too. Caleb was looking in the opposite direction from the sign in the gazebo as they drove past it, and Billie didn't point it out to him. He'd hear about it all tomorrow from the guys at the quarry, no doubt. For now, it would just make him worry about her the way her dad had.

"Now Mitch wants me to find out who or what killed the three of them, or else he's going to expose me to the town and tell them I did it," she finished as they pulled up in front of the cabin. She waited for some response from him, but he got out of the car without saying anything. Billie blew out a long breath and then followed him. She'd been relieved to have the chance to tell him, finally, to fill him in before Mitch tried to turn him against her. But she couldn't tell what he was thinking, now that she had.

Caleb stood just inside the door, unlacing his boots, then tossed one heavily in the general direction of the shoe rack.

"That *asshole*," he said once Billie shut the door. Billie relaxed a little. He was on her side, then. He tossed the second boot and it dislodged a pair of Billie's shoes from the rack. He headed straight for the kitchen. "You know what? We should just leave. I am so sick of him controlling our lives like this. I have cousins on my mom's side in Denver we can stay with until we figure out where to go. But we do *not* have to stay here and put up with this."

In a small voice, Billie said, "*You* don't."

"You don't either."

Exasperated, she said, "I can't shift outside of Juniper! If I leave, I lose that part of myself."

"Have you ever tried?"

"No! My mom told me I could only shift here, you know that."

He heated random leftovers and ate them standing in the kitchen, saying nothing for a long moment.

"Billie," Caleb said, his voice now patient, calmer. "I want you to consider something, without getting mad about it, okay?"

She narrowed her eyes at him, promising nothing, but he pressed on.

"You were a kid when your mom told you that, right? And parents don't always tell their kids the whole story. What if—just hear me out—what if when she said you couldn't shift outside of Juniper, that was a rule, like, you weren't *supposed to*, rather than a limit, like you wouldn't be able to?" He paused for a moment while Billie tried to make sense of what he'd just said. "Maybe she was just trying to make sure you wouldn't end up getting lost or in trouble or something. Like when my friends would come over, my mom used to tell us we couldn't leave the cul-de-sac. That didn't mean we literally couldn't if we tried."

"But she told me..." Billie sat on the couch, and hugged her knees up to her chest. She struggled to remember exactly what her mother had told her. One of the strongest memories was of a time she'd taken a school field trip down to Denver, when her mother had repeatedly told her she couldn't shift down there, that it was out of her territory. She *had* left then, but she hadn't even thought about shifting the whole time she was on the trip. "But what if, I don't know, what if I try, and it kind of breaks something, so then I can't do it anymore. Or what if I hurt myself just by attempting it?"

"Your mother wasn't from here, right? But she could shift here."

That was true, and the fact threw her off for a moment. But then she remembered something and shook her head.

"She used to talk about some initiation that would happen when I was a teenager," Billie said. "But I didn't get that. Maybe that's like a ritual or something that lifts the boundary."

She'd forgotten all about that. *Was* that what the initiation did? Expand or remove the territorial restriction? She couldn't remember—it was one of a dozen things her mother had promised to explain when she was older. One of the many secrets that disappeared along with the smoke of that shotgun blast.

Caleb sighed. "You're not going to let me take you away from here, are you?"

Billie shook her head.

"You'd rather let *him* throw you to the mob." Caleb rarely said *my dad*, or even *Mitch*, as though speaking his name would tether him to this man he had such disdain for. He set the used dishes in the sink. From there, his back turned to her, he asked, "Did you do it?"

Billie blinked a couple of times before she managed, "What?"

"I mean, is it possible that you did it without realizing it?" He turned to look at her now, his face hard. Her heart sank.

"Shapeshifters aren't the same as werewolves, Caleb, I've told you this before. I'm in complete control of what I do when I'm shifted." She had no idea if werewolves actually existed, but she'd seen the movies, the gruesome transformations under moonlight, villagers rallying to rid the world of this monstrosity, the horror of being bitten and turned against your will. Her mother had shown her a couple of those movies when she was too young to be watching them, in order to impress on her the danger of letting others know what she was. *This is what they'll think you are*, she'd said. And she had been right. Even the one person she thought she could trust thought she was a monster.

"I know you say you're in control," Caleb said, "But isn't it possible? Like, if there's a conflict between what your human side wants and what your animal side wants, the animal might just take over?"

"No," she said. "They're not 'separate sides'. It's more like… like putting on different types of clothes. Like wearing flimsy sandals or sturdy hiking boots. They're both shoes, they just function differently. One works better than the other depending on what you need."

She couldn't even believe they were having this conversation. He might end up siding with Mitch against her after all, if Mitch told him she was the killer. She hid her face in her arms, wishing she could hide in her quiet dark cave until all of this was over. Caleb crossed the room and pulled her into his arms. Reluctantly, she leaned against him, melting into his familiar warmth. His touch usually softened some of the pain she always carried around, but there was too much of it right now.

"I believe you," he whispered.

"No, you don't." Billie almost choked on the words.

He tipped her chin and looked her in the eyes. "Yes, I do," he said firmly.

She trusted him. She couldn't help but trust him, the way he looked at her.

"We're not going to let him scapegoat you."

Billie pulled away from him and flopped heavily onto her side on the couch, punching a pillow. "Either I solve the mystery and clear my name, or I find some way to blackmail him back. I don't see any other way out."

Caleb shrugged. "Most of his dirty laundry isn't exactly hidden."

"Yeah, but no one will air it because everyone works for him."

"Not everyone," Caleb said.

"Right," Billie said, trying to keep the bitterness out of her voice. "Working at the quarry rather than for him so that he demands you pay back the college tuition he paid for is a *much* better solution than actually working for him."

"Keeps me out from under his thumb."

*Not really,* Billie didn't say, because she knew he already knew it.

Instead, she told him about the human footprint at the crime scene, and her suspicion that it could be another shapeshifter. But if there was a mechanism to lift the territorial boundary, like the ritual she had just remembered her mother talking about, then that meant that if there was another shapeshifter in Juniper, they *weren't* necessarily a local. That sure expanded the suspect pool.

"If it was a shapeshifter tourist," Billie said, "they could already be gone. There's no way to know who it was."

Caleb snapped his fingers. "I know! You could ask the Casino Ghost."

Billie sighed. "You're really a lot of help today."

"No, seriously, I used to talk to him when I lived at the hotel. Maybe he can tell you if someone weird has passed through there." Billie stared at him for a moment, before he turned to her and said, "What?"

"You used to talk to the Casino Ghost."

"Yeah. Every now and then, I'd see him on the top two floors. He liked me, for some reason."

"You're talking about Reno Bridges."

"Duh," Caleb said. "I've told you about this before."

"I always assumed you were just joking around."

"Really?" He feigned hurt. "You thought I was just bullshitting? These were tender memories of my troubled adolescence."

"Well, yeah, I assumed you were bullshitting," Billie said, "Because ghosts aren't real."

Caleb laughed. "You're a *shapeshifter*, Billie."

"Yeah, but… that's not the same thing."

"I can't believe you don't believe in ghosts. Weren't you leading the ghost tour a couple of days ago?" He checked the time on his phone. "You'll have to try to catch him in the middle of the day, though. He hides when there are too many people around. That's why most ghosts get spotted in the middle of the night. They get, like, skittish around most people. Since the casino's busy all night, he's more likely to be out when no one's around in the middle of the day."

"Are the other ghosts real? The janitor, the woman in white…?"

Caleb shrugged. "I never saw any of them. Reno's the only person who's ever actually died at the Silver Coin, as far as I know."

Billie stared into space, her head swirling. If ghosts were real, and they hung out at the place where they died, then was it possible that Frankie and Gil and Toby were still lingering in Toby's driveway, lurking among the surrounding trees like spectral deer? Or—her breath caught in her throat—was it possible that her mother was still haunting the house on Shadow Ridge? She tried to swallow the lump that formed in her throat. No, that kind of hope hurt too much. And she still wasn't convinced the Casino Ghost that Caleb had seen was anything more than a vivid dream or a stoned hallucination.

"If you're messing with me," she told him, "I'm going to claw your eyes out."

"These eyes?" He blinked flirtatiously at her, which came across much more as silly than sexy, but succeeded in breaking some of the tension. She tossed a throw pillow at him.

"I mean, I can't guarantee you'll see him," Caleb said, "but Reno Bridges *does* exist. Tell him I said 'what's up.'"

# WEDNESDAY

The next morning around eleven, Billie rode the Silver Coin elevator next to a tourist woman who held a small apricot-colored poodle against her shoulder. A dog like that in the mountains was likely to become coyote food the first time the owner looked away. Billie was surprised Mitch even allowed pets in the hotel. The poodle was far too small to be a shapeshifted person, but Billie scrutinized it anyway, as she had every animal and person she'd seen this morning. The dog sneered its lip at her, baring tiny needle-like fangs. The woman chastised the dog and apologized profusely to Billie.

Dog and woman got off at the third floor and Billie continued up to the fifth floor. When the elevator carriage stopped, she entered the code. The doors opened on the empty casino. The room's tall, narrow windows were covered, with only a half-moon sliver at the top of each to let in light, and not much of it, at that.

Caleb hadn't said if the ghost needed darkness. She could go get a flashlight from the check-in desk and do this ghost hunt in the dark, but there was no guarantee that a swinging flashlight beam would be any less threatening to a ghost than a full ceiling of lights. Or she could shift, use her feline night vision to explore the casino, and just make sure to get out or shift back before anyone else showed up.

Even if that solved the problem of *seeing* the ghost, in bobcat form she would have no chance to communicate with the ghost if she did find it. The room smelled like stale smoke and lingering body odor. She'd never been here as a cat; the layers of smell would probably be overwhelming. Her human nose wrinkled just thinking about it. She took a chance and hit the lights. They buzzed on, flooding the room in florescence.

Billie stood in front of the closed elevator doors as the lights finished flickering all the way on. Her shoes seemed to sink into the casino carpet. The hydraulic whir of the elevator dissipated, leaving only the humming of the lights.

Billie took a step forward into the empty room. With the second step, a cold breeze brushed over her arms. Her heart rate increased, and she stopped, took a breath to try to slow it. A draft didn't mean a ghost. That sudden breeze could have been a lot of things. Totally natural, normal things. She took another step, and that's when the chime of a slot machine split the silence.

Lights danced on a machine three rows in. The clunk of the lever echoed beneath its tune. Billie inched quietly toward it, goosebumps already pocking her arms. The lever clunked again, and the reels spun with a steady whir. One thudded into place, the second, then the third. The lights flashed and sound effects trilled to announce a jackpot, but no coins fell into the tray. Billie reached the end of the row.

A man hunched on the stool. Vertebrae pressed through a thin, white shirt. He reached up and pulled the lever again. As Billie quietly moved closer, the pattern repeated. Three thunks and a celebration of lights and chimes. She stopped, only one machine between her and the hunched man. Slowly, he swiveled his head until it tilted over his shoulder, revealing a bloated, greenish face, eyes pure white with no irises. Coins filled his open mouth, dropping out and falling to the casino floor.

Though her first instinct was to run screaming, Billie swallowed her fear, clenched her fists at her sides and stood firm.

"Reno Bridges, I need to ask you some questions," she said.

The man disappeared and the slot machine died, the lights fading and chimes swirling into a discordant finale. The ghost reappeared behind Billie, a smoke-like hand snaking over her shoulder. She whipped around and stepped backward, knocking over one of the stools. It clattered against a slot machine and then rolled across the carpet.

"I'm not afraid of you," she said.

Her nervous system disagreed, but she held her ground. Strangely, she felt no urge to shift, and she took that to mean that this was a purely psychological fear, not a physical threat. The ghost disappeared again and the whole row of machines flashed and chimed in a violent cacophony.

"Caleb… Caleb Mulligan says to tell you 'what's up,'" she tried, feeling dumb, and wishing Caleb had given her some kind of actual message for the ghost.

The machines shut off, leaving the room silent for a moment. Then came a sudden chill as the ghost wrapped figure eights around her legs, coiling up her body.

"You are different, aren't you? Not fully human, or at least, not like most other humans." His ghostly face stopped inches from hers; a smoky tail looped around her waist. "What are you?"

Billie hesitated, then said the words she was never comfortable saying out loud, had only said to someone else a couple of times. "I'm a shapeshifter."

"Ah, yes," the ghost crooned. "There used to be more of you. Rare these days, quite rare."

Billie's throat clenched. He knew. He could tell when someone was like her. The ghost inspected her for a second longer, then unwound from her waist and sat on top of one of the machines, tendrils coalescing into a more solid form, legs crossed and dangling in front of the machine's reels. His trousers had sharp creases, and he wore a tipped fedora. He might almost look like a normal man in a 1920s costume, except for the fact that he was perched implausibly on top of a slot machine. He spread his hands as if to tell her to proceed. The movement left smoky trails.

"Are there others… like me… in this town?"

"None but you have passed through my domain in years, dear girl. But these walls are my cage, you see." He reached arms out to either side, and they stretched and dissipated like smoke rings, then came back together as arms again. "What goes on out there in your world, I could not say."

"Did you know my mother? She's been gone for a long time. Her name was Valerie." She spoke the name with quiet reverence. Ghosts must be rare too, especially those as substantial as Reno Bridges— otherwise they'd simply be accepted as fact instead of legend. But Reno *was* real, and that meant there was a possibility, however small, that her mother's ghost existed too. What if she had been haunting the house on Shadow Ridge for all these years, waiting for Billie to come find her? The thought made Billie want to race out of the Silver Coin that very second. Forget Mitch and his unreasonable demands.

"Time," the ghost was saying, "is not quite the same for me as it is for you." He was starting to fade, becoming more translucent, and though she still had a million questions, she realized she might be running out of time to ask them.

She cleared her throat, tried to focus on why she was here. "If I say Gil Gorman and Frankie Cokes, do you know who I'm talking about?"

"Two of Mr. Mulligan's henchmen, aren't they? The older Mr. Mulligan, I mean. Dreadful fellows."

"Yes. They're dead."

"Well, they didn't die in here. And I'm afraid I don't have a telegraph line to other ghosts, my dear."

"No, that's not what I meant," she said. "Do you know anyone who might have wanted to kill them?"

"Plenty, I'm sure."

"Specifically. Or if you've heard anything that could lead to who might have done it…" She trailed off, feeling hopeless.

The ghost shook his ethereal head, and the movement created a blast of frozen air.

Billie sighed. "What about—" But before she could get anything out, the ghost dove off the top of the machine and swooped behind her, cold mouth close to her ear.

"There's only one thing that motivates both the living and the dead: hunger. The only question is what you are hungry for."

The ghost burst apart and faded like fog burned off by the sun.

"What are you talking about?" she yelled.

The florescent lights hummed loud in her ears again. The slot machines had all fallen silent and the ghost was nowhere in sight.

She'd waited in the casino nearly half an hour longer, but Reno Bridges hadn't returned. Down in the car, Billie shook her arms as though wisps of the ghost's essence had stuck to them. *Yep, ghosts are definitely real,* she thought, staring into space and trying to calm the chill that wouldn't let go of her bones despite the warm summer air. *If only the couple in the ghost tour had seen what I just…*

They were meeting with Robyn to possibly buy Billie's childhood home. The house where she'd just realized her mother's ghost could still be. Was that today? She checked the time on the car's dashboard. Wednesday afternoon, that's what Robyn had said. Assuming the couple hadn't run screaming back to Denver yesterday after discovering the bodies in Toby's driveway, of course. Billie drove back across town and down Miners Avenue, slowing as she passed the real estate office. Robyn's Subaru wasn't parked in front. Billie turned on the next street and followed it up the curving path toward Shadow Ridge.

Aside from one trip with her grandmother to collect some belongings, Billie hadn't been back to her childhood home since the night her father had fired that shot. What if her mother had been there all along, roaming the house in the moonlight, waiting for her daughter to return?

At a bend of the road, where runoff had cut miniature canyons along the shoulder, raspberry bushes grew. Billie remembered walking with her dad down to corners like these every childhood summer, both of them carrying a plastic bucket, eating as many raspberries as they took home, their hands both stained pink for days. She wanted to pluck him out of that happy memory and replace it with her mother, but no, it had always been him, every summer until they didn't have summers together anymore. Just like it had always been him who had driven her from house to house on Halloween, which was the only way most kids in the mountains could trick or treat, since the ground was too icy in October and most of the houses were too far apart for a costumed child to walk between them. Billie had always disliked Halloween. Pretending to be something else, she could understand, but a bit of makeup or a plastic mask didn't fool anyone. Her dad loved it, though, so she let him pick her costumes: a princess, a cowboy, a witch, an astronaut. And even though she usually started the night grumbling, she would always end it laughing as he told silly monster stories while they drove from house to house. Then they'd go home and dump the candy on the living room floor to sort through it.

The old house came into view. A real estate sign poked out of the packed dirt at the end of the driveway featuring Robyn's face, her company's logo, and her phone number. The house had been painted since Billie had last seen it, the formerly blue siding now a sickly green. It looked much smaller than she remembered, but wasn't that always the way when encountering something you'd known as a child? Even her father himself; she'd remembered him as a towering hulk, but the man who'd come to her door was frail and thin, and hardly taller than she was.

Billie sat in the car for a moment. Probably, she'd missed them. Maybe she'd just peek through the window, see if she could glimpse anything supernatural. It was quiet here, tranquil like the empty casino. Caleb had said ghosts got skittish with too many people around. If she stepped lightly, cat-like, maybe she'd see something. If there was even anything here to see.

But just as she opened the car door to step out, a shiny red Subaru pulled into the driveway and parked behind her.

"Here we go," Billie mumbled.

The ghost had said that hunger was the only thing that motivated the living and the dead, and Billie thought there was some truth to that. Billie's hunger for connection with her mother, and Robyn's hunger for wealth and status had led them to the same place today. And the young couple who followed Robyn out of the car, what hungers drove them? Billie wondered mildly, but she didn't really care. The woman, Chloe, had seemed nice enough when she talked to her at the Silver Coin bar, but she was just another outsider. There had been an odd exchange of residents over the last decade: most of the neighbors Billie had known on this road from childhood had moved *to* the city, and most of the people who lived here now had moved up *from* the city. Or from some other city in Texas or California. She knew the ones who lived here year-round, but a lot of these houses were second homes, occupied only a few months out of the year, or vacation rentals with a never-ending rotation of occupants.

"Well hello, Miss Blackwater!" Robyn said with awkward formality, surprise clear in her voice. She wore a light blue skirt that hit her knees and a navy blue blazer with retro-style shoulder pads that looked terribly uncomfortable. Chloe stepped out next. She wore a white peasant blouse and fashionably distressed jeans, but it was the flip-flops with faux rhinestones on the straps that really made her look out of place. The man—Billie struggled to remember his name—wore khaki shorts and a plain t-shirt. A few years ago, Billie would have said they stood out up here in the mountains; now, people like them were the new face of Juniper.

Billie lifted a hand in awkward greeting. Chloe gave her a confused look, but then covered it with a genial smile and said, with mock reproval, "Are you stalking us?"

Billie shrugged. "Small town."

"It is that," Chloe admitted.

"I'm kind of surprised you're still out here looking at houses," Billie said. "After what you found yesterday."

Chloe's face darkened. "It was horrible. But we have more positive memories of this little town than bad ones, don't we, Luke?"

Luke had his head inside the Subaru, where he was digging through a large bag. A streak of rusty red stained one of the cargo pockets of his shorts. Billie stared at the stain. The ghost had said no shifters had passed through the casino, but if he was confined to the top floors, that meant he didn't know who was in the rest of the hotel. And Chloe and Luke definitely hadn't been granted access to the casino. Would Billie even be able to recognize another shapeshifter if she met them? Would there be some way that, like the ghost, she would *know* they were different? It had been so long since Billie had been around another shifter that she didn't even know.

They had been the ones to find the bodies—could that have simply been a way to keep the suspicion from falling on them? But the scent signature around the footprint had indicated someone who was malnourished, the scent of hunger so strong that their body had started to burn through its own muscles. Luke didn't fit that. If anything, he was a little chubby, and had that soft suburban look of someone who worked behind a desk, someone who had never known true, desperate hunger. For food, at least.

Billie turned back to Chloe. "What do you think killed them?"

Chloe looked puzzled. "They said it was an animal of some kind."

"Is that what it looked like to you?"

Chloe shuddered. "I think it had to be. I don't see how a person could do all of that."

Robyn said, "Excuse us for just a minute," and grabbed Billie's arm, steering her away from Chloe. Billie flinched away from the unwanted touch, but Robyn kept hold of her arm. "*What* are you doing here?" Then her expression darkened and she took a few steps closer, saying in a lower voice, "Wait, you're not working with a different real estate agent, are you?"

Robyn looked like she might claw out the eyes of this fictional adversary as soon as she encountered them. Billie considered telling her "yes" just to see how upset she'd get about it.

Instead, she said, "Please let go of my arm," a dangerous edge to her voice. Once Robyn let go, Billie said, "No. I just wanted to have a look inside the house, if that's okay with you."

Robyn's expression instantly brightened. "So you're reconsidering my offer, then?"

Billie sighed. "I don't know if you remember, but this house was where I lived, before…"

"Oh!" Robyn said. Then, "*Oh*. I thought that had been torn down." She cleared her throat. "Let's not bring up that history in front of my clients, okay?" Chloe and Luke were fawning over the wildflowers in the front yard. Robyn turned toward them, then quickly back to Billie, her eyes narrowed in suspicion again.

"Don't mess up this sale for me. If they pass on it, I'll hold this property for you until we can talk, but I *guarantee* they have better credit than you."

In Robyn's world, that was probably a hefty insult. And, Billie realized she'd given Robyn the impression that she might be interested in buying the house. Well, if her mother's ghost really was here, maybe she would be.

Robyn switched back into sales mode and called Luke and Chloe over while she opened the electronic lockbox on the front door.

Luke was walking around with his phone in the air. "Is there no service up here?"

"Cell coverage is still spotty in some places in the mountains," Robyn explained. "That's why we have to use these old-fashioned lockboxes up here, too. Can't have a client locked out just because some Bluetooth wouldn't connect."

"It's good, honey," Chloe said. "We spend too much time on screens anyway."

Luke grumbled and put his phone away, following Chloe and Robyn into the house.

To Robyn, Chloe said, "Everyone's way too reliant on technology. That's one of the things I like about up here, it's almost like going back in time a couple of years."

The house was vacant, and the interior had been completely remodeled. Billie couldn't recognize the pattern of knots on the wood floor, or the trim on the doors and windows. She couldn't point out where the sofa used to be, or where the table had been where her mom had shown her how to fold paper animals, or the exact place in the second bedroom where she had crouched naked and crying, waiting for the police to arrive. The memory was vivid, but she couldn't map it onto this remodeled physical space. She followed Robyn around the house, listening to her chatter about the age of the pipes and the amount of counter space. Their shoes left footprints on the dusty floor, and a spider web caught in Billie's hair as they entered the master bedroom. But for all the ambience, there was no sign of a ghost. Was her mother more likely to haunt the house where she'd lived with her husband and daughter, or the yard where she'd died? Did a ghost *need* walls to contain it?

Billie cleared her throat, and took a chance as the group wandered back into the living room. "Have previous occupants of this house ever reported any strange sightings?"

Robyn glared at her. "No, of course not. I have no idea what you mean."

"Maybe they *want* a haunted house." Billie winked at Chloe, who broke into a grin.

"We *are* amateur ghost-hunters, you know," she informed Robyn.

"See?" Billie said, gesturing expansively with her arms.

Robyn's mouth opened and closed a few times, and she stuttered a moment longer before she got her bearings and said, "Well, no, I don't think you'd find anything like that here. But some of our local residents do claim to have seen a Bigfoot in the area. And there's certainly plenty of wildlife, in any case. As you can see, this backs right up against National Forest…"

Robyn led the couple out into the backyard. This time, Billie didn't follow them. She waited until Robyn's heels stopped clicking against the wooden floor, until the back door slammed shut behind them, and she stood alone in the empty living room. The energy of the others' presence faded and everything became very still.

"Mom!" she whispered, and the word made her throat clench. "Are you here?"

She felt no cold breezes like she had at the casino, saw no strange movements. She moved toward the bedrooms, and lingered in the hallway just between them.

"Mom," she whispered again.

She couldn't even bring voice to the words. The hope that she wasn't fully gone, the grief that Billie might have had access to her all along and didn't realize…

What if her mother had haunted the house for a year, or for ten years? What if at some point the curtain had opened for her to move on? However that worked. What if Billie had already missed any chance she'd had? A gold streak of sunlight painted the floor of the room that had been Billie's old bedroom, and she watched the dust swirl, waiting to see if it would coalesce into a ghost. It was selfish to wish for one last glance, to hope her mother's spirit *had* been stuck here for so many years. Selfish, yes, but she couldn't shake the wish.

Outside, Robyn screamed.

Billie raced through the house, bumping into walls, tripping over the kitchen threshold, and flung open the back door, just in time to see a raccoon scurrying into the trees. Robyn stood in front of a small shed, one hand on her chest. She laughed, a loud, wheezing sound almost as abrasive as the scream.

"Oh my," she said to Chloe and Luke, who were practically squealing with delight from their close brush with nature. "There must be a hole in here somewhere. We can see about getting that fixed."

Billie sat down in the sole rocking chair on the back porch to compose herself, letting the adrenaline settle, making sure her bones all stayed the same shape. The porch and the overgrown yard felt more familiar than the house. It wasn't a yard like people in the city had, with uniform grass and a fence to mark exact boundaries. This was more of an oblong meadow surrounded by trees. Yellow dandelions sprouted between shin-high grass stalks and thick patches of crabgrass. A clump of blue-purple columbines swayed on their thin stalks right where the trees began. This was where she and her mother used to leave their clothes when they shifted. This was the forest where they had been free to be themselves.

Billie looked out and tried to remember exactly where her mother's body had lain. She rose from the rocking chair and stepped through the tall grass to the center of the meadow. Kneeling, she touched her palm to the ground.

There were no scars on the earth to reveal the trauma that had occurred here, no marker to commemorate. But this was undoubtedly the place where it had happened, where the body had fallen. Billie grabbed a stick and stabbed it into the hard ground so that it poked up, one dead thing in the wild living garden. Like a thin wooden headstone.

Her mother had been buried in Juniper's small cemetery. None of her mother's family had come to the funeral—no one knew how to contact them. On the first anniversary of her death, Billie had ridden her bike to the cemetery instead of going to school. She'd found the tombstone graffitied with pentagrams and upside-down crosses. After that, she'd never gone back.

Robyn was talking again, and her voice was like sand lashing across Billie's face. She tapped Billie on the shoulder, saying she was heading back to her office and Billie should call her later. Billie pushed her out of the way, and stalked out into the forest. She didn't get very far before she squatted onto her heels. Her eyes ached from the sunlight and she pressed the palms of her hands into the ache and let great heaving sobs roll through her chest. There were no thoughts, just fragments of sound, slashes of color, and the overwhelming sensation of her human form and its animal longing. She wasn't afraid she might accidentally shift—in fact she felt trapped in her human skin, as though she'd lost any possibility of ever being something else. Robyn might have been standing there watching her. The whole town of Juniper could have been yelling at her and she wouldn't have heard a word. For the moment, she had disappeared into herself.

"Fold it like this," Billie's mother had said, matching corners and giving the paper a confident crease. Billie had tried to copy her, clumsy six-year-old fingers finding a sloppy approximation of the sharp lines and tight folds. Still, when she'd held out the lop-sided paper fish, her mother had clapped her hands together and declared, "Very good!"

Her mother took the fish, and held it up beside her eyes. "But it's not a fish, even if it looks like one, right?" To Billie's dismay, she unfolded her creation, smoothing the paper across the table. "It's just paper," she said as she deftly folded a different pattern. "And it can be—" She set the paper, now in the shape of a duck, on the table between them. "—anything it wants to be."

"Anything?" Billie asked reverently, picking up the paper duck.

"Well," her mother said. "Lots of things, anyway." She was folding another sheet now, making something new. "You have to know where to put the folds, which edges to pinch, which sides to match. But you can learn a lot of different shapes." She set an elaborate fox on the table now, standing up on four pointed paper feet.

"Like us," Billie said.

"Just like us," her mother agreed. She picked up one of Billie's books from the floor, a collection of paper dolls, and gently pressed the seams to punch a new one out. She held up the doll, a blonde girl standing in underwear waiting to be dressed in cardboard clothes. "Most people, they're like this doll. Cut out. Stiff. You can put whatever clothes you want on her, but she's still always going to be a doll. And if you try to fold her, she'll just break." She flexed the cardboard to show how it wouldn't fold. "But we're different. We're special. We're not stuck in one shape. Our bodies fold."

"Can I be a dinosaur?"

Her mother had smiled. "I've never seen one before. Maybe you'll be the first. But—" She picked up the duck again, held it up beside a fresh sheet of paper. "Remember that the paper can always be folded into something smaller than itself, but it can't ever be stretched into something bigger. If you try, you might rip the paper, and then it can't go back together again."

Under the forest shadows behind their house, with her mother there to guide her, Billie had tested out the folds and creases of her unusual body, found what hurt and what felt right, found some of the limits of what she could and couldn't create. No dinosaurs, and no wallabies or monkeys either, though she repeatedly tried. No lizards or chipmunks—small was fine, but those were too small, it seemed. But a coyote, a bear cub, a scruffy dog: these she could manage, even if only with the same clumsiness as her paper fish. She managed an owl once, but though she stretched and flapped her wings, she couldn't get off the ground to fly.

"Sometimes it depends on the size and shape of the paper," her mother had said one time when Billie couldn't quite accomplish a deer shape. "And you still have a long way to grow."

Years later, in high school Biology class, Billie had learned something about the way DNA proteins fold, and how the shape of those folds meant as much as the information contained in the DNA itself, and it had almost made sense to her. But then, nothing about the world had made much sense since her mother had died and left her alone in this world full of cut out dolls.

A soft hand touched Billie's back, and for a moment she expected to look up and see her mother standing over her. But it was only Chloe. Billie fell out of her crouched position, landing awkwardly, and rubbed the tears from her eyes.

"It's the anniversary of something I don't really care to remember," she explained. It wasn't, not quite, but it seemed a natural reason she might be out here crying over something years gone.

"More bad memories than good," Chloe said, nodding.

"No," Billie said. "Just… one really bad one that burns the edges of all the others."

Chloe extended her hand. "It's about to rain."

Billie waved the proffered hand away and stood on her own. They started back toward the house. The first drops of rain landed heavily on her arms, and the two women ran to take shelter on the porch. Luke and Robyn were already in the Subaru. Mountain storms moved fast. Air pushed up over those fourteen thousand foot peaks often spun into clouds that turned dark within minutes, and by the time you saw them, it was almost too late to get out of their way. Chloe and Billie stood on the porch together, watching the sheets of rain.

"My son died," Chloe said suddenly, and Billie looked over at her.

"I mean, it was a miscarriage, no one ever told me a sex, but a little boy came to visit me in a dream, and I know it was him. He said the world was just too hard and he would be too soft to handle it. All of us who live in this world have to become hardened too. After that, though… the city started to feel *too* hard for me, like I'm being poked with the sharp edges everywhere I step."

So there it was, Chloe's hunger, laid out bare.

"I wish I could tell you grief gets easier," Billie said.

Chloe gave her a sad smile. "I wish you could, too."

"If you're trying to get away from hard edges," Billie said. "I don't know if you really want to move here. Winters are brutal. People are… people. There's drugs and crime and…" She trailed off before voicing the word "murder."

"I know," Chloe said.

*Do you, though?* Billie thought. "Juniper isn't some idyllic village," she said.

Chloe sat in the rocking chair, but jumped up with an "Oh!" almost immediately.

"What is it?"

"It's cold," Chloe said. "Ice cold. Just there. Can't you feel it?"

Billie swallowed, and reached toward the chair, the hairs on her arms prickling. Was it just the chill of the rain, or something more? But just before her fingers met the wood frame, the chair began to rock.

Billie and Chloe both stepped backward. There was a light breeze, but not enough to move a chair, especially in such a rhythmic motion. This wasn't the same rocking chair they'd had when Billie lived here. That one had been inside, and it had been dark brown wood, with stickers she'd put all over the legs. This one was probably left by the most recent residents, made of lighter-colored wood, the varnish peeling off from being left exposed to the elements. It kept rocking, emitting the faintest creak from the porch's wood slats. Billie took a tentative step forward, and the rocking chair came to an abrupt halt.

"Mom?" Billie whispered, the word barely managing to escape her tight throat. She searched the shadows, waiting for her mother's face to form in a misty figure like the Casino Ghost. He had been so vivid, almost corporeal. "Mom, please, I need to talk to you."

The ghost, if that's what it was, remained hidden. Billie waited, hugging her arms and trying to smooth out the goosebumps on them. Chloe remained silent, standing still as though trying not to startle a wild animal. The rain started to let up. Billie was just about to suggest they head to the cars. She could come back another time, maybe at night, alone.

But then the rocking chair moved again. Billie stopped, turning toward it. She still couldn't see any ghostly forms, but the chair appeared to move of its own accord. The rocking increased speed, becoming urgent, almost violent.

"Ohmygosh," Chloe yelled, just as Billie saw something flash in the window: a reflection of a human-like figure moving between the trees.

She spun toward the forest, but whatever it was had disappeared. The rocking chair abruptly stopped.

"What was that?" Billie whispered.

"I don't know," Chloe said. "It was upright, like a person, but something about the shape of the torso was… wrong."

Something told her that what they'd glimpsed in the forest definitely wasn't her mother's ghost. Her skin rippled, a fear that she didn't fully understand quickening her heartrate.

"We should get out of here," Billie said.

Chloe nodded vigorously. She looked scared, but also excited, a mix of emotions that Billie pretty much shared. She readied her keys, and they ran toward the cars. Billie locked the doors as soon as she was inside hers. Her hand shook as she turned on the ignition. Had Luke or Robyn seen whatever that thing was? She doubted it. But Chloe had. And she'd seen the rocking chair moving as well.

The rain beat against her windshield, roared down the driveway. Any remaining evidence Billie might have been able to find about Toby, Frankie, and Gil would be washed away by this rain. She'd squandered a whole day chasing ghosts instead of solving the mystery Mitch had demanded she investigate.

Yes, there was something left of her mother in that house, even if it was faint. But there was something else out there, too.

When Billie got back to the cabin, Caleb was home early from the quarry, though it looked like he had just arrived. His hair was dripping from the rain. He stood barefoot, the lower legs of his jeans soaked, and he was wringing out his t-shirt in the kitchen sink. Billie shut the front door behind her, a ripple of thunder joining the thick pattering of rain. She pushed the damp strands of hair out of her face and Caleb looked up and grinned at her, and suddenly nothing else mattered. She crossed the room to him, snared fingers through his belt loops and stood on her toes to kiss him, pressing herself against his slightly damp chest. He kissed her back hungrily, and lifted her up to sit on the kitchen counter, making her face more even with his, and she wrapped legs around his waist to draw him in close.

They made their way to the bedroom, their intensity matching the intensity of the storm. Once the storm outside had calmed, they fell asleep in a tangle of limbs, the rain still drizzling.

Billie woke up disoriented, and it took her a moment to identify the buzzing sound that had woken her. She extracted herself from under Caleb's arm and he rolled over with a sharp inhale and a loud yawn. Fumbling with the clothes on the floor, she finally extracted her phone and flipped it open.

***Where the hell are you?*** A text from Mitch. No, a dozen texts, the same message or slight variations of it. Billie looked at the time—she should have been at the Silver Coin an hour ago. She groaned. There were a dozen other people in town who could work the hotel's bar; she was completely disposable as far as that was concerned. People who could do it better, too, who wouldn't have customers complaining about drinks poured too strong or not strong enough, who would flirt back and make them feel welcome rather than just ignore their comments like Billie did. Her ability to shift, to spy for him: that was the only thing that made her necessary. And it's not like a plethora of alternative jobs waited for her in town if Mitch decided he was done with her. Much as it pained her to admit, she needed him.

Caleb sat up and snaked an arm around her shoulders, kissing her neck. "Stay," he whispered.

Another duplicate message buzzed in. Billie flipped the phone shut.

"I can't."

"Tell him you're on the case," Caleb said. "You can't come in because you're tracking down a really hot lead."

Billie giggled and pulled away from his warm breath on her neck. She shook her head.

"And then what do I tell him when he asks what I've found? I've got *nothing*. I'm no closer to figuring out what's going on, and I have two more days until he throws me to the wolves."

"No one's going to believe him," Caleb said.

"He'll probably hold me at gunpoint and force me to shift in front of everyone."

"He wouldn't..." Caleb started to say, but he trailed off, no conviction in his voice. "Do you really think you're going to get any closer to an answer by pouring whisky sours for mid-week drunks? *Stay*, Billie. I just want to have one normal evening together. We never get that."

Billie wanted that too, more than anything. A life without Mitch controlling their every move, conspiring to keep them apart, lording Caleb's debt and Billie's secret over them. A life where they could have dinner together, go to bed at the same time, go grocery shopping together, watch movies together, have friends, maybe even have… She shook the fantasy away. She *could* have that if they left her territory behind. But then she would be just another cut out doll, like everyone else.

"But everything's *not* normal." She slid out of bed and pulled dry clothes out of the wardrobe. "I can't. I'm sorry."

Caleb rolled onto his back. "Tell him I said 'fuck off.'"

"Sure," Billie said. She gave him a kiss and then headed out the door. As soon as she sat down in the car, she realized she hadn't told Caleb about Reno Bridges, about going up to Shadow Ridge, any of it. They were supposed to go talk to Brock so Billie could find out what he'd seen; that had been the original afternoon plan. But she had needed his touch so badly. Caleb's touch helped to wash away the echoes of everyone else who had touched her recently: Mitch shoving her onto the couch; her dad gripping her shoulders; Robyn grabbing her arm; Chloe attempting comfort. Spending the afternoon in bed might have seemed indulgent, but it had been the healing she had needed. She hesitated, hand on the ignition, wanting to go back inside, but then her phone buzzed again. ***Clock is ticking, kitty cat.***

She texted Mitch back: ***otw***

Then she started the car and drove away from the cabin.

Hardly anyone was at the Silver Coin that night. She saw Chloe and Luke pass through the lobby. Mitch stalked down from his office to verify that Billie was, in fact, standing behind the bar, but he didn't demand any answers from her. Which was good, considering she had none to give him. Just more questions. Like, what the hell had she and Chloe seen? The Bigfoot that Mouse was always talking about? Or the shifter Billie suspected, glimpsed in some half-transformed state? Was it the same thing Brock had seen at the quarry before his accident? And would the hunters who were looking for a killer mountain lion somehow manage to stumble across it?

The rain picked up again. Billie leaned against the bar, gazing out the windows at the dark branches whipping in the storm. She regretted that she hadn't stayed home with Caleb. At least if the teams of hunters were still out there in the forest, holed up in their tents or blinds, they were getting drenched by the storm. It was a small comfort knowing they wouldn't get their scapegoat kill—not tonight, anyway.

The few patrons who stopped by for a drink mostly said things like, "Sure hope this passes by the weekend," and "Not going to be any fireworks if this keeps up."

Then Heather slid onto a stool and ordered a martini. Heather owned the Enchanted Mountain Metaphysical Shop, which specialized in angel statues, crystals, and other new age paraphernalia like dreamcatchers and palm reading books. Heather was in her early fifties, a little older than Billie's mother would have been now if she'd lived. Billie had gone to her once as a teenager to ask what she'd known about her mother, but although they'd had a nice long talk, Heather had offered no indication that she knew anything about Valerie's abilities. When Billie had broached the subject of cryptids like shapeshifters and werewolves, Heather had handed her a book that to Billie's disappointment only viewed shapeshifting as a metaphor, using animal imagery in meditation to access your inner strengths. Still, Billie had always liked Heather, and that's more than she could say for most people in this town.

During the slow spell, Billie had folded about a dozen bar napkins into origami flowers. Heather pointed to them and said, "Ooh, can you make me a lucky crane?"

"I actually never learned how to do the crane," Billie admitted as she shook and poured the martini. "Picking up Kim?" Kim was Heather's wife; she worked at the Silver Coin's check-in desk.

Heather nodded. "Guess she's tied up with some large party reservation on the phone."

"Fourth of July," Billie observed. The craziest time of year in this town, and it was coming up this weekend.

"It's all that keeps us from becoming a ghost town, I suppose," Heather said as she sipped her martini.

"Speaking of ghosts…" Billie started, but Heather's genial expression melted to annoyance.

"I wish you'd all leave that poor dancehall ghost alone and stop pretending like the Silver Coin is full of others. The only reason I haven't helped him move on yet is because he asked me not to. But those ghost tours you guys run here are just nonsense. They discredit the hard work that real investigators do."

"I…" Billie started, unsure how to react to Heather's unexpected rant. Had she been the only one who didn't know that Reno Bridges was a real ghost? Did *Mitch* know? "No, I know," she started again, and Heather's expression softened. "I agree with you. But I was wondering… not everyone who dies becomes a ghost, right?"

"Imagine how crowded the world would be if they did?"

Billie leaned forward to peer out into the lobby, gauging how much time she had with Heather to ask the dozens of questions she had. Kim was still on the phone, the cradle pinched between her ear and shoulder as she typed reservation details into the computer. Before Billie could get her next question out, though, Heather was already talking again.

"Most ghosts aren't like Reno, though. Intelligent hauntings are kind of like wild animals—even if you know they're in the area, you're likely to catch only a glimpse of them, if that. They keep away from people. I think we scare them as much as they scare us. But Reno's more… domesticated. Like a coyote who's gotten so used to people he'll come right up and beg for food."

"Sorry, did you say 'intelligent' haunting?" Billie said. "What does that mean?"

"Sure, it means that he has some awareness of the corporeal world. He can speak, he can interact. It's sort of, though not quite, like he just kept on living without a body. Most hauntings are residual. That means it's not necessarily a soul that's trapped between worlds, more like an imprint of the person's energy. Usually they just replay either the trauma of their death or some mundane moment of their life on an infinite loop."

Billie hoped whatever presence was lingering at the Shadow Ridge house wasn't that second kind. She wanted her mother to be there, but not if it meant she had been reliving her own death for so many years.

"Is there a way to, like, call up a ghost?" Billie asked. "Are séances real?"

Heather laughed. "If it were easy, imagine how convenient that would be for police work? We might be able to find out the real story of what happened to Toby and Daniel."

Billie was about to ask her next question when she suddenly realized what Heather had said. "Wait, Daniel too?"

She realized she hadn't seen Daniel Gadbury since the night she'd followed him out to Toby's, not even in the big crowd Randall had gathered at the gazebo.

"No one can find him," Heather said. "He's not answering his phone. His mom says his place is totally trashed and he's nowhere to be seen. With the killer lion, or whatever it is, everyone's assuming the worst."

"Shit," Billie breathed.

Kim walked in then, and Heather slid off the barstool to give her a kiss. She left the mostly un-drunk martini on the bar.

"Wait, a mountain lion wouldn't trash his house, though," Billie said, her mind still reeling.

Heather shrugged. "That's why I think we might not have the whole story. Just be careful out there," she said. "Don't go anywhere alone."

"Yeah, you too," Billie said, half paying attention, her mind already racing.

The bar remained vacant after Heather and Kim left. Billie ran through a list of people she might call to ask about Daniel, but couldn't formulate an excuse for why she might be looking for him. She switched the TV in the corner of the bar from whatever reality show it was playing and searched the channels for a news report. She watched one for a while, but they were discussing oil prices and wars in the Middle East and stock market fluctuations—far off things that felt like they had no bearing on her life. She found more local news that ranged from a domestic violence incident to new construction along I-70 to several missing college students in Boulder. Nothing about a missing 30-something man in an isolated mountain town. She'd just need to go over to his place tomorrow and see for herself what she could find.

# THURSDAY

In the morning, Billie woke to the smell of bacon. She crawled out of bed and stood at the doorway between the bedroom and the living room/open kitchen, rubbing her eyes. Caleb glanced over his shoulder.

"You're still here," she said. Normally he was off to work before the sun rose. It was late enough for the sun to be up, though the light was still dim, last night's storm lingering.

"Quarry's closed today." He slid the bacon onto a plate next to some eggs and toast, and held the plate out to her. She stepped forward to take it.

"When did you get groceries?" There hadn't been much left in their kitchen other than a few cans and a bunch of condiments. Caleb usually bought the groceries because he preferred the larger store in a nearby town about twenty miles away, rather than the tiny and overpriced local store.

"Before you woke up."

Billie breathed in the scent of the bacon, her mouth watering. "What would I do without you?"

Caleb shrugged. "I dunno. Hunt birds, marmots. What do bobcats eat, anyway?"

"Rabbits," Billie said absently.

"Have you eaten a raw rabbit?"

"Once," Billie admitted. "But I got really sick. Apparently shifting doesn't overcome that whole 'not being able to digest uncooked meat' thing humans have."

"Gross," Caleb said, but he was smiling. He kissed her on the forehead, then sat next to her at the small table with his own plate.

Over breakfast, Billie filled Caleb in on everything that had happened the day before: the casino ghost, the speculation about her mom's ghost, the news that Daniel was missing. She ended by trying to describe what she and Chloe had seen in the forest behind the Shadow Ridge house.

"Brock said he saw something before his accident, didn't he?" she asked.

"He did."

"I'd like to go talk to him," Billie said. "And maybe stop by Daniel's after that and see what we can find out."

Caleb hesitated a moment, frowning, but then he said, "Yeah, I should check on Brock anyway." He downed the last of his coffee and went to get dressed.

The rain had let up, finally, and the clouds cleared, leaving a pure blue sky. On the drive to Brock's house, Caleb said, "So we might find out something here, or we might not. If not, what's your plan?"

Billie realized he was probably asking if she was willing to leave town, but she chose to defer that answer by deliberately misunderstanding him. "Reno Bridges suggested we do a séance at the site where Frankie and Gil died, see if we can ask them what happened ourselves."

That wasn't what he'd said at all, but she thought the idea might sound more credible coming from an actual ghost.

Caleb stuck his lower lip out and nodded. "Could work, I guess." Billie had no idea if it would work, but she was getting very short on both ideas and time. A moment passed before he said, "And if it doesn't?"

Billie said nothing. Her shapeshifting territory had been the main thing keeping her here, but now there was also her mother's ghost in the Shadow Ridge house. Even if she was willing to give up her shifting, she couldn't leave before she got the chance to go back to the house, find out if she could talk to her mother like she'd talked to Reno. It might take time to coax the ghost out of hiding. She thought maybe she would talk to Robyn about selling the cabin after all, and see if there was a way to buy the Shadow Ridge house back without going too much into debt. But she wasn't sure Caleb would be okay with that plan at all. Later. They could talk about all that later.

Tara sat on the front porch, leg bouncing in nervous agitation. She looked up expectantly as the car pulled into the driveway, then visibly drooped when only Caleb and Billie stepped out.

"Hey, Tara," Caleb said. "Is Brock inside?"

"No!" The word came out as a whine. "He's gone. I don't know what happened."

"He couldn't have gone far with that broken leg," Caleb said.

"He didn't *go* anywhere," she said. Her knee bounced even higher now. "Something took him. I know it. That's what predators do, they pick off the sick and the injured."

"So he was running with a herd?" Billie said.

Tara looked at her as though startled to learn that Billie could speak, and Billie glanced down at herself to make sure she was, in fact, presenting as fully human. Then Tara's face crumpled in confusion. "What?"

Billie cleared her throat. "Never mind. Did you find anything out of place?"

"He left his *phone* here," she said.

"That doesn't mean anything," Caleb said. "Brock would forget his own head if it wasn't attached."

Tara looked baffled again. "But it's his *phone*."

Caleb kept asking Tara questions: When was the last time she saw him? What was the last thing he said to her? Who else could they call who might have seen him? Why didn't she want to tell the police he was missing?

Billie knew the answer to that last one, even though Tara bumbled through it. Caleb had said they'd found Scarlet in Brock's bloodstream, and based on Tara's bright red face and the bad-sunburn flaking on her arms, it was pretty clear she'd been taking it too. She looked worse than two days before when Billie had seen her—then, she'd assumed the redness was from crying over her injured partner. Now, Billie had little doubt about the cause.

Billie wandered around the side of the house, still listening to Tara's answers, but searching for anything unusual: a splash of blood or an odd bare footprint, for example. She was around the back, checking the ground near the rain barrel, when a new car pulled up. She rounded the corner to see who had arrived.

Tara raced toward the car. Brock hobbled out of the back seat, adjusting his crutches so he could stand on them. Billie recognized two locals in the car's front seats. The one on the passenger side passed a joint to the driver and gave a peace sign as the car pulled out of the driveway.

Tara banged her fists on Brock's chest, nearly making him lose balance on his crutches.

"Where *were* you? Why would you leave like that? I didn't know where you were, something could have happened to you—"

"Whoa," Brock said. "Chill out. I went to get some stuff."

"What *stuff*? You know there's a killer out there, you can't just leave—"

"Chill out!" he practically yelled while she continued ranting and hitting him. Caleb kept reaching toward her and then stopping, as though unsure if he would make things worse. Billie took Caleb's hand, gave a small sharp shake of her head.

"Here," Brock said. He produced a vial of red liquid from a pocket. "I got some shit for you, too."

Her entire demeanor instantly changed, and she seized the red vial with a squeal of delight. Brock hobbled toward the house, nodding a belated greeting to Caleb and Billie. Tara uncorked the bottled and upended it into her mouth.

Brock stopped. "Don't take the whole fucking—" He sighed, nearly growling in frustration. "Damn it, Tara, I can't drive your ass to the hospital when you O.D."

Tara leaned forward, hands on her knees and head hanging, her hair draping down over her face. She flipped her head up and Billie let out an involuntary gasp. Was it a trick of the light, or had the irises of her eyes turned red along with her face?

"Hey, man," Caleb said to Brock. From the nervousness in his voice, Billie assumed he'd seen her eyes, too. "How, uh, how long have you guys been doing this stuff?"

Brock hefted his cast-laden foot up the last porch step.

"I dunno, couple weeks, I guess. She's the fiend for it. Makes me feel fuckin' weird, like I don't belong in my own skin."

*Fiend was right,* Billie thought. Tara staggered around the driveway like she was drunk. At least she wasn't trying to knock down trees like Frankie and Gil had.

"You know how much it takes to O.D.?" Caleb asked. He was clearly spooked.

Brock gave a grunt and a shrug.

"Frankie and Gil each took half a vial," Billie said.

"And they're dead now," Caleb retorted, "so that's no comfort."

The skin of Tara's arm rippled in a way quite similar to how Billie's did before a shift. Billie glanced over at Brock and Caleb, but neither of them appeared to have noticed it.

"Hey, Tara, let's go inside," Billie said.

Tara ignored her, spinning in circles with her arms wide.

Brock let the screen door slam behind him, but Billie and Caleb stayed where they were, watching Tara spin and sway.

"Must be a hell of a drug," Caleb said. "Wonder what it feels like."

"I have *no* desire to find out," Billie said. She was watching for that ripple across Tara's skin again, but all she could see was that it was growing redder by the moment, that same deep sunburn-type rash that had afflicted Daniel's face the night Billie followed him out to Toby's.

Finally, Tara stopped spinning and plopped down cross-legged in the middle of the driveway. She held her arms out to the sides and looked at them as though surprised to see them attached to her body, then started worrying at a flake of skin on her left forearm, picking at it with fingernails. Brock hobbled back out onto the porch holding two beers. Tara pulled at another flaking piece of skin on her arm, just above the wrist. This one, she kept pulling, the transparent blister getting longer and more opaque. By the time it reached the elbow, it was clear she was just tearing skin.

"What. The. Hell," Brock shouted. The beer bottles clattered onto the porch and he hurried down the steps as fast as his crutches would let him. Billie and Caleb both just watched dumbfounded as Tara yanked the layer of bloody skin free and let it drop to the ground. She crawled away from Brock, and tugged at another loose spot on her upper arm, exposing raw muscle beneath.

Maybe there had been no animal attack at all, Billie realized with horror. Toby and Frankie and Gil all might have clawed their own bodies apart because of the drug.

But just as she'd decided that's what must have happened, something crashed through the trees behind them and Billie whirled toward the sound. She reached out and grabbed Caleb's sleeve in a fist just as something charged across the driveway toward them.

The creature's body shape was generally human, but its muscles were bulked and swollen in odd places, and something that looked like the buds of undeveloped wings sprouted from its back. And it was red. *Bright* red, like exposed muscle, or fresh blood.

"What the fucking hell is that?" Caleb yelled, at the same moment Brock said, inexplicably, "I told you—fucking forest lobster!" He slipped on his crutches and fell. Caleb rushed forward to help him get back onto his feet.

Pointed nostrils sniffed the air urgently, then the creature turned crimson eyes on Billie, who instinctively took a step back. Then its gaze landed on Tara. Her eyes went wide and Tara scrambled to her feet. It charged.

Tara took off running into the forest, the creature on her heels. Billie raced after them. Caleb shouted her name, but she didn't turn back. Though the creature was fast and the forest was thick, she could see the flash of red between the trees ahead, could hear Tara's terrified shrieks. Billie stripped as she ran, leaving a trail of clothes on the forest floor until she was free enough to shift, then bounded forward. Her bobcat body was quicker, more efficient. Nothing about this encounter was safe, but she had a better chance against something like that creature with teeth and claws than with thumbs and voice.

The only catch was that in bobcat form, her daytime vision was dulled. The vibrant red of the creature that had been so easy to see with human eyes was washed out now by her feline colorblindness, appearing a shade of green that practically blended in with the forest. But the creature's scent trail was strong and distinctive, so she let that sense guide her.

She skidded to a stop when the smell of blood flooded the air, strong and coppery, along with the sour odor of urine. The creature crouched behind a bush, and it—oh god, it looked like it was eating. Billie crept forward, trying to get close enough to see what she really didn't want to see. The creature lifted its head and turned toward her, a bit of intestine dangling from its mouth. Billie froze, one paw hovering in the air, too shocked to flee. It bent down again, took one more bite from Tara's lifeless body, and then darted off into the trees.

Caleb called her name again. Billie groaned, but in bobcat form it came out as a strange half-caterwaul. *Why* had he followed her? Why had he put himself in danger like that? She glanced the direction the creature had gone, but turned back toward Caleb's voice instead.

Caleb stopped short when he saw her loping toward him. He'd gathered up most of her discarded clothes and clutched them in front of him with both hands.

"Billie?" he asked unsurely. He had seen her in bobcat form before, but only a couple of times.

Billie unfolded herself back to human form and stood up.

"Oh, wow," he said. "That was—that's the first time I've ever actually *seen* you shift. That was totally freaky."

She grabbed the clothes he held and started to pull them on. "You know what else is freaky? That thing out there that just attacked Tara."

"Is she—" But even as he said it, his eyes landed on the foot sticking out from behind the bush. He dropped Billie's shoes.

"Shit," Caleb said. He ran a hand through his hair, turned in a half-circle, looking around the forest.

Billie pulled her pants on, leaving her shoes on the ground, and grabbed his arm. She caught a glimpse of the full mess of Tara's body then. Billie's stomach didn't heave quite the same as when she'd seen Toby in his driveway. Amazing, how quickly one could become accustomed to death and carnage.

"Come on," Billie said, pulling him away from the body. "You need to get out of the forest. Now."

"Me?" Caleb said, halting. "No, you are *not* going after that thing again."

"I have claws." Billie mimed a claw shape with her hands, going for levity, but Caleb was having none of it.

"No, we need to get the hell out of this place. That thing—that's a job for, like, a professional monster hunter, or an exorcist, or something. We need to just get far away."

"What, and leave it to slaughter the rest of Juniper?" Billie yanked her arm out of his grasp. "I know you never really considered this place your home, but it *is* mine. I'm not going to walk away from the town with a monster running loose."

Caleb shook his head. "So what are we going to do?"

"I don't know, but right now, let's get out of the forest, tell Brock what happened to Tara, and call Mitch so he knows what's really going on."

Billie headed back toward Brock's house, but Caleb pointed toward the body.

"What about—what do we do with…"

"Break the news to Brock, and then figure it out from there. Let's go."

As she led Caleb out of the forest, Billie's mind was racing. The creature had chosen to go after Tara, even with Brock there, clearly injured and easier to target. All of the previous victims had been men: Toby, Frankie, Gil, and probably Daniel. But each of the victims did have one important thing in common, Billie realized: they'd all been on Scarlet.

Billie whispered this theory to Caleb on the way back to Brock's house.

"So, what," Caleb said. "Someone takes too much, they start attacking other people who have taken it?"

Billie nodded grimly, remembering Tara's intestines hanging out of the monster's mouth, and Toby's hollowed-out torso. She hadn't seen Frankie and Gil's bodies, but she'd be willing to bet their stomachs had been eaten, too.

"Drug addiction doesn't turn people into literal monsters," Caleb said.

"Maybe this one does," Billie said. "Remember how Tara was peeling her skin up just before it attacked?" And that ripple across her arms, which no one else had noticed. Maybe this drug triggered the same gene or chemical reaction or whatever that led to shapeshifting, transforming their bodies into that strange red creature.

"When Brock was almost attacked at the quarry, he'd been taking it then, too." Caleb shivered. "Okay, so then who is it?"

"I don't know," Billie said. "Elliot Moran, maybe? Toby's cousin, that's who normally hooks him up with drugs. Toby was killed the night his new shipment came in. Elliot or someone with him could have dosed with him when they delivered, and that was the tipping point." Had there been a couple of vials missing from the tray she'd taken from Toby's house? It made sense. As much as any of this made any kind of sense. Ghosts and literal monsters hadn't been part of her reality a few days ago, but here they were.

Caleb banged on the door and Brock opened the curtain to see who it was before letting them in. Billie already had the phone to her ear, calling Mitch.

"Brock," she said when Mitch answered, "I need you to tell Mitch what you saw."

She shoved the phone at him.

"What?"

"Tell him what you saw out there."

"It was a goddamn devil. A demon. That same thing that started to come after me at the quarry."

"Take the phone."

He snatched it from her with a grumble and held it to his ear. "Hello?"

"What the hell is going on?" Mitch yelled loud enough that Billie could still hear him even though Brock had the phone now.

Brock gave a bumbling recount of what had just happened, then held the phone back out. "He wants to talk to you." Billie took the phone back. Before she could lift it to her ear, Brock asked, "Where's Tara? Is she okay?"

Billie looked to Caleb to signal that he needed to be the one to deliver the bad news to his friend, then lifted the phone and walked into the other room, putting a finger to her other ear so she could hear Mitch.

"Did you get all that?" she asked him.

"Not really. The hell is he talking about some red devil?"

"Thought you might appreciate a third-party witness so you know

I'm not just trying to save my own skin."

"But you are trying to save your own skin, aren't you?"

"I'm trying to save all our skins." Literally, Billie thought with a shudder. She wished she could stop seeing the image of Tara yanking at the skin of her own arm.

Billie explained what she'd seen and how she thought it was a person transformed by taking too much Scarlet, feeding on others who had recently dosed on the drug.

"So where is this 'creature' now?"

"I don't know."

"Then go find out!" Mitch yelled. She hung up without saying anything more and crossed through the living room, waving to Caleb to follow her out to the porch. He left a distraught Brock on the couch.

She went around the side of the house and started to take her clothes off.

"You're not really going back out there?" Caleb said.

"I have to track where it went. And if I'm right, then it won't attack me because I haven't taken Scarlet."

"And if you're wrong?"

"I'm not wrong." She held the clothes out to him, and when he didn't take them, she suddenly felt more naked and vulnerable in front of him than she ever had. Did he look at her differently now that he'd seen the shift happen in front of him? She should have waited, should have gone behind a tree or something. There was nothing beautiful about the transformation, she knew, and she didn't want the one person in the world who found her beautiful to think of her body folding in on itself next time he reached for her. But it was too late; he'd seen, and she couldn't control how he reacted to what he'd seen. "Take these," she insisted, "and meet me back at the cabin later. Please."

Reluctantly, he took the clothes from her. "But how will you…? I mean… are you just going to come scratch at the back door when you're done?" He didn't know that she had a stash of extra clothes at the cave near the Silver Coin, and in the abandoned building next to the cabin. She bit her lip, debating whether to tell him. It didn't matter that he knew, but it was her last secret. What if somehow he slipped and told Mitch? Then she'd have no place to hide from him if she ever needed to.

"I have a some clothes hidden," she settled on saying, without elaboration.

She glanced around, but there was nothing she could easily hide behind to change. So she met his gaze, as though challenging him not to be disgusted by her, but Caleb turned away as her body melted into the shift. She gave one last look over her furred shoulder at him, and then took off into the forest.

Tara's corpse lay in the same spot she'd found it before, crawling with bugs now. The ground around the body was scuffed with footprints: hers, Tara's, Caleb's. She parsed the air for the monster's scent signature, managed to separate out one that led off to the north. She followed it. Male, adult—not quite as malnourished as before, but not healthy, either—intertwined with that sharp scent like dry red wine mixed with blood that she'd noticed at Toby's house. The scent of Scarlet.

The forest was crisscrossed with the scent signatures of hunters. Several groups of them, from what she could tell. Damn, she'd forgotten about them. She was supposed to stay *out* of the forest until they were done with their killing frenzy. But she kept to the monster's scent trail despite the risk. A couple of footprints pocked the dirt along the way, these ones bigger, less human than the original she'd found near Toby's driveway. Almost like it had a large dew claw now, and a wider base, the sole of the foot padded or callused.

The scent led back toward Daniel Gadbury's house, and seemed to circle it a couple of times. Billie kept her distance from the house, but she could hear someone talking loudly on a cellphone. She could hear and smell half a dozen people on the property. Billie positioned herself out of sight, but close enough she could catch occasional snippets of conversation.

Daniel's mother was apparently calling people from his phone, since she had to introduce and explain herself with each call before asking the other person if they'd recently seen her son. The others, Billie didn't recognize, likely family or friends from out of town. After listening to several calls, Billie repositioned herself to try to see the front of the cabin, and managed to get at least a glimpse of the yard. Daniel's truck was in the driveway.

Odd, that the monster had left all of the other bodies, but not Daniel's. Also odd that the monster would return to this property today, when it had likely attacked Daniel several days ago. Unless…

There'd been something bothering her ever since she guessed that the monster could be Toby's cousin, Elliot Moran. It *didn't* actually make sense that he'd attacked after they'd dosed on Scarlet together when Elliot brought the new batch. Toby had been attacked while trying to enter his house. Yet the Scarlet vials had been safely inside already.

Billie stopped in her tracks, sniffing to see if she could parse any other information from the area, but it was too mixed with the scents of everyone else who had been at Daniel's house.

If she was right, then the monster was a person who had been transformed by the drug. She recalled how red Daniel's skin had been the night she followed him, how upset he'd been that Toby was out of Scarlet. If he'd been missing since the night Toby was attacked, it seemed a pretty good guess that Daniel was the one who had transformed. Daniel was the one who had attacked Toby, and all the others.

As Billie worked out this logic, another truck rolled up in Daniel's driveway, and out stepped Randall Briggs and several of the other hunters who had joined his quest to eradicate the supposed killer mountain lion. One of them dropped the tailgate to let out a leashed dog who instantly started sniffing the ground. Billie shrank back a few steps, her fur bristling. The dog was mixed breed: lean and long-legged, with brindled brown fur, a long snout, and folded ears. Randall was telling Daniel's mom that if he had fallen victim to the killer cat, it might still be in the area. Daniel's mom insisted he might still be found passed out in some degenerate friend's house, based on all the drugs they'd found in his cabin. Her tone was sort of mock angry, as though she would be perfectly happy to find him in a gutter. After all, it would be possible to get her son back if he'd just gone on a drug binge. But if that drug was Scarlet, and it really did transform people the way Billie suspected—was there a way to recover from that? Once he'd turned, could he turn back?

Billie kept her eyes on the dog as she slowly backed away. It sniffed at the ground some more, then suddenly raised its head and gave a couple of sharp, short barks.

"What is it?" one of the hunters said, and she could smell their spike of adrenaline. The dog barked again, and loped in her direction.

Billie took off through the trees as fast as she could.

"Get it!" she heard the hunter say. The dog's paws beat the earth behind her.

Her heart pounded. Humans, she could outrun, easily outwit by disappearing into the landscape. But a dog would be able to follow her scent. She changed directions, heading toward a ridge where she might be able to climb the rocky cliff and hide in one of the caves or crevices. Neither the dog nor the humans would be able to follow her up that.

But before she could reach the ridge, the dog gained. The animal's breath was hot on her back. She leaped, claws digging into tree bark, and scrambled upward. The dog jumped; lucky she didn't have much of a tail, or it would have been caught in the dog's jaws. She tucked the small nub of her bob-tail down, climbing higher. When she'd climbed as high as she could, she perched on a branch that was almost too thin to support her.

The dog stood on hind legs at the base of the tree, scratching at the trunk and barking. The men gathered around the tree's base.

"It's a cat, alright." One of the men aimed a gun upward. Billie looked around for an escape route. There was one tree that might be close enough to leap to, but it would be a risky jump. If only she could shift into a bird—it had been years since she'd tried the owl form and had never managed to fly in it, so she would probably fall from the sky and land right at their feet if she tried. Besides, she'd never shifted from one animal form to another without going back to human first. You had to unfold the paper before you could refold it, didn't you?

"Yeah, a bobcat, you doofus," Randall said, putting a hand on top of the barrel to encourage his friend to lower the gun. "Look how small it is, nothing more than an overgrown housecat."

Billie curled in, trying to make herself look even smaller. The effort caused the branch to groan beneath her.

"I say we take it out anyway," said a third man.

"Don't be an idiot. You shoot now, it's just going to scare off what we're actually looking for," Randall said. He leashed the dog, and offered it a treat. The dog swallowed the treat in a slobbery gulp.

The men argued over Billie's fate for a few moments longer. She felt her skin ripple the same as it had done when she'd lost her dog form a few days ago. She concentrated on keeping the shape. If she shifted back to human now, she'd surely break the branch and land naked at their feet, probably with a broken neck, too. She wasn't safe as a cat; she wasn't safe as a human. She desperately wished she *had* learned to fly.

A whistle sounded through the trees, and the man who'd still had his gun trained on her lowered his weapon. The three men headed back toward Daniel's. Billie stayed put until their voices faded, then she crept to a sturdier branch and waited there a few more minutes before she climbed all the way down.

Halfway to the ground, she lost control of her form and fell, landing on a bare human back, the pine needles that coated the forest floor jabbing at her vulnerable human skin. She lay there for a moment, staring up at the treetops and the bits of blue sky peeking through them, unable to catch her breath or still the shiver that wracked her.

She rolled to her side and sat up, hugging her knees to her chest. Eyes closed, she focused, then landed on four paws again, back in bobcat form. Strike three for shifting in a potentially visible location. And the second time she'd lost control of holding her animal form. Maybe she was losing that part of herself anyway, even without leaving her territory. Or maybe it was just nerves, a confusion of that fight-flight-or-shift instinct that couldn't decide whether she was safer as a human or as a cat.

She wanted to get back to her cave as quickly as she could, but she steeled herself. Follow the scent trail, find out where the monster went. Then, once she had that information, she'd stay the hell out of the forest until the hunters were finished with their crusade.

She followed the scent trail until she reached a nearly sheer cliff. Shadow Ridge. Her childhood home and her mother's ghost were a quarter mile from the summit of that ridge. At the base, she stopped and looked up at it. She'd been heading here to escape the hunters, but now that she looked at it, she realized she wouldn't have been able to climb very far up it, even as a bobcat. She sniffed along the base, but no, the scent definitely went straight up. The creature she was tracking *had* managed to clamber up the seemingly unscalable cliff. She backed up, scanning the rocky face.

A flash of movement drew her eye to a shadowy enclave. The creature—or rather, Daniel Gadbury, now transformed into this creature—was hiding out in a cave up there.

After Billie shifted and ran back out into the forest in her mad pursuit, Caleb stuffed her clothes into the backseat of the car and went back inside. Brock was slumped on the couch, his injured leg propped on the coffee table and crutches haphazardly tossed on the floor. He stared off into space.

"She's gone, isn't she?" he said, and it took Caleb a moment to realize that he meant Tara and not Billie.

Caleb opened his mouth, but nothing came out. The sight of Tara's shredded body was burned into his mind. He tasted bile at the back of his throat just thinking about it.

Apparently taking his silence as confirmation, Brock put both hands over his face.

"*Shit*," he said, the word muffled behind his hands. He kicked the coffee table with his uninjured leg, causing the table to move enough that his injured leg slipped off of it, and then he cursed again.

"We should call the cops, probably," Caleb suggested.

Brock groaned as he hefted his foot back onto the table. "No, dawg, are you crazy? I don't want cops up here. You think they'll believe a word of what we saw? Not a chance, dawg, they're gonna be pointing at me and you."

"Trust me, when they see what happened to her, no one's going to suspect you did *that*."

Brock put his hands over his face again. "Her dad's gonna kill me. He already hates me. He's literally going to drive up here and put a gun in my face."

"We have to do something," Caleb said.

"Bury her."

"What?"

"Let's just dig a hole and bury her. We can tell everyone she's missing, like Daniel Gadbury. The only ones who know what really happened are me, you, and Billie." Brock sat up then and looked around, startled. "Shit, where'd Billie go?"

"She…" Caleb hesitated. Brock didn't know about Billie's shapeshifting. After what they'd just seen, Caleb was tempted to just tell him, but that was her secret to reveal or not.

Brock pointed angrily toward the forest. "Is she out there? With that thing? Why'd you let her go?"

Caleb shook his head. "You know Billie. I don't *let* her do anything, she does what the hell she wants."

"Gonna get her ass killed just like…" Brock trailed off and slumped back onto the couch, unable to say his wife's name.

"She thinks it's only attacking people who have taken Scarlet." Brock considered this information in silence. After a while, Caleb tried again: "We should call somebody."

Brock shook his head vehemently. "No. We should bury her."

"We?" Caleb gestured to Brock's bum leg. But after a moment, he sighed. "Okay."

Maybe, Caleb thought as he dug the grave, he should have waited until his friend wasn't so much in shock. Maybe he should have called the police anyway. Maybe he should have gotten in the car and just driven east, and farther east, until there were no more mountains. Maybe… maybe… With each shovelful of dirt, a new maybe, with each stab of the shovel into the earth, a new regret. But he dug, trying to get deep enough that the grave wouldn't attract coyotes, bears, or mountain lions. No accounting for forest lobsters or drug-crazed demons, but he sure hoped that whatever that thing was they'd seen, it had no more interest in the body.

When he started to sweat, Caleb took off his shirt and draped it over the blood-splattered wild rose bush. Digging was hard work, but he was strong from his time at the quarry, physical labor he never dreamed he'd end up doing when he'd enrolled in those business classes in Boulder. *For Billie*, he thought, and hoped she was safe out there, that she wasn't going to be the next one he buried. He shook his head. Brock was a good friend, but not someone he ever thought he'd be willing to bury a body for. *For Billie*, he thought again, and it became the mantra that got him through the rest of the grave.

Bugs had swarmed over Tara's face now, and once he had a deep hole, Caleb stood there leaning on the shovel, staring down at her.

He'd never known her very well, hadn't really liked her, but he wouldn't wish this fate on an enemy. Well, maybe on his dad, he thought bitterly, and immediately regretted the thought. No, not even on him, shithead though he was.

There was a rustling, and Caleb spun around, suddenly aware of how exposed he was out here. Human witnesses could wander off a nearby trail, or the monster could return for a second meal. But the sound was just Brock, hobbling awkwardly through the trees. Before Caleb could stop him from getting close enough, Brock's eyes landed on Tara's shredded body. He didn't react, just stared. His eyes were glassy and red, and he smelled like a combination of whiskey and marijuana.

"Have you ever seen a dead body before this?" Brock asked suddenly, raising his eyes to Caleb.

"Yeah," Caleb breathed. "My mom. She had cancer, and I was there when she passed."

She had looked awful—bald and shriveled and sunken, a shell of the woman who had pushed him on a tire swing or ridden bikes with him along the Highline Canal. He'd seen the light leave her eyes, the breath leave her chest. And he'd sworn, though he'd never told anyone this—not even Billie, not even his dad—that he'd felt her hand on his shoulder just an instant after she was gone, that he'd seen her standing behind him. But the vision had vanished as soon as he turned to get a better look.

Caleb shook the memories away. "You?" he asked Brock.

"No," Brock said. "I mean, yeah, some animals of course. And my grandpa, I guess. When I had to go to his open-casket funeral when I was a kid. But that was… different."

*Different.* Yeah, that was for sure. Caleb looked over Tara's body again. He leaned on the shovel, wiping the sweat out of his eyes.

"There's still time to tell someone," Caleb said.

Brock stared a moment longer, his face hardened, a muscle twitching in his jaw. "She wouldn't have wanted anyone to see her like this," he said finally.

So, Caleb dragged the body into the grave and Brock watched as he shoveled the dirt back into the hole. When he was finished, Caleb scattered some pine needles and aspen leaves over the top, but it wouldn't fool anyone. He could only hope that the rain and wind and grass would render the grave less obvious over time. That they would have that time before someone came looking. Caleb waited to see if Brock would say anything, a prayer or eulogy or something, but Brock just stared at the spot a moment longer, then said, "Thanks, dawg," and hobbled back toward the house.

Caleb followed, leaving the shovel leaning against the side of the porch. Inside, he washed his hands and face in the kitchen sink and put his shirt back on, though it clung sticky to him.

"You okay here by yourself?" he asked Brock. He knew the answer was certainly no, but he desperately wanted to go home and take a shower, maybe rethink all of his life choices. And find out if Billie was okay. Brock would likely just drink himself into a stupor tonight, and Caleb could check on him in the morning. Brock waved him away, assuring Caleb he was fine, already pouring another tumbler of whiskey.

Caleb's desire to wash the day away was thwarted as soon as he pulled up in front of the cabin. A man sat on the porch, and even if Billie hadn't given him a heads up that her father was out of prison and back in town, Caleb would have guessed that's who this was. They had the same close-set blue eyes, the same spatter of freckles across nose and cheeks, the same straight, wispy hair, though his was dark gray rather than light brown, and it was thinning around a widow's peak. Even the way he sat, with one ankle crossed over the other knee, was identical to how Billie often sat. It was creepy, how similar they were. He'd never tell Billie that, of course, but it was true. Caleb sighed and got out of the car.

"Billie's not here," he said as soon as he'd shut the car door. He wasn't sure that was true. She could have made it home already, but if she had, she clearly didn't want to talk to the man on the porch.

"I know," the man said, standing to meet Caleb halfway up the walkway. "But I heard she had a boyfriend. Was hoping to talk to him. That you?"

"That's me," Caleb said wearily.

The man extended his hand. "Keith Blackwater."

Caleb didn't accept the handshake, more because his hands were blistered and sore than because of an intentional snub. He climbed the porch steps and plopped heavily into one of the porch chairs. "I know who you are."

Keith joined him in the second plastic chair. "You know what she is? What she can do?"

Caleb hesitated, but then said, "I do."

She'd shifted right in front of him this morning, and he didn't even have the words to describe what he'd seen. *Grotesque*, kept coming to mind, *unnatural*. But also *extraordinary, magical*. He wasn't sure if he wanted to watch it again a thousand times or forget he'd ever seen it. Though the more he thought about it, the more he was actually leaning toward the former. It had been incredible to see something like that with his own eyes.

"Wish I had known," Keith said, and Caleb didn't offer any response to that. After a moment of awkward silence, Keith cleared his throat. "There are others, you know."

"Here?"

"No." Keith shook his head and gestured toward the road out of town as though waving away their current location. "Out there. I met some in Durango. That's what I want her to know. She might never forgive me, but I want her to know she's not alone."

"She isn't *alone*." He shot Keith a glare.

"I mean…" But before Keith could elaborate, either to justify what he'd said or dig a deeper hole—Caleb inwardly cringed at the metaphor, vowing not to use it again—Keith trailed off, watching a truck putter along Miners Avenue. Some of the hunters Randall had gathered rode in the bed, banging on the side of the truck while the driver honked the horn. Between them in the truck bed, hung on a stick like a roasting pig, was a very large, very dead mountain lion.

Once back in her cave, Billie stayed in bobcat form for ten more minutes, curled up in the dark, the walls of her cave like a loving embrace. Her one safe spot. It seemed it was becoming more and more risky to be an animal. There were so many people now, even in this small town deep in the mountains, and if Mitch and Robyn got their wish to expand local tourism, there would be more flooding in all the time. Would there come a time when Billie had no isolated space to shift in, no place in the forest she could run without a person seeing her? How long until some summer camp group discovered her cave? How long until there was a sun-bleached landmark sign at the base of this hill, just like all along the trails? How long until the forest was sold off and divvied up into plots, new houses every few feet?

When she encountered the hunters the second time, she was back in human form and on her way toward town, dressed in the last set of clothes she'd had in her cave: jean shorts and a long-sleeve sweatshirt too warm for early July. The hunters looked at her as though she were odd and out of place—which was often true no matter where she was—but said nothing. This wasn't the same group that had treed her earlier, but she was tempted to hiss at them all the same. They appeared to be heading back to whatever trailhead or dirt road they'd left their vehicles parked at.

Caleb wasn't inside when she walked through the cabin's back door. He should have been back by now, though, right? It had been a couple of hours since she'd left Brock's. Maybe he'd had to stay and give statements to the police about Tara. She wondered what they would agree to say. At this point, police involvement was only going to complicate things, no matter whether they lied or told what they'd really seen.

She opened the front door and Caleb was there, slouching in one of the chairs. His shirt was sweat-stained and his pants were covered in dirt. Billie started to ask him about it, but stopped short when she noticed the person sitting next to him in the other cheap plastic chair.

Her dad gave her a sad smile and raised a hand in greeting.

"What the hell is he doing here?" Billie hissed.

Caleb pointed down the street. "Think we've got bigger problems right now."

She stepped out and followed his gaze to the throng of people choking Miners Avenue, and the dead mountain lion skewered and displayed in the back of a truck parked near the gazebo. A news van was trying to navigate through the crowd to park.

Billie groaned. "Oh no, they did it."

She let the door shut behind her and rushed toward the crowd.

"Billie, don't—" Caleb reached for her as she passed him, but didn't quite catch her, and didn't stand up to follow her.

"...may face misdemeanor charges for off-season hunting..." one of the news reporters was saying into a camera as Billie passed.

Randall Briggs leaned against the gazebo, megaphone in his hand and a smug expression on his face as though he'd just finished a speech. A line of men, as well as a couple of women, jumped into the truck bed to kick the lion's corpse or take selfies with it. Billie looked away in disgust.

Mitch stood in the shade next to Enchanted Mountain. He was the only one aside from the reporters who wore formal clothing: a black suit, his hair slicked back with gel, looking the part of the mob boss he liked to act like he was. Billie caught his eyes and he winked at her. She frowned in confusion.

A familiar and irritating voice pulled Billie's attention back to the crowd. Robyn was preening in a pocket compact mirror while the reporter and camera person readied the best angle.

"I can't say I condone how it was done," Robyn said into the camera, "but I am very glad that the threat to our wonderful community has been neutralized. And just in time, too! Our Fourth of July festivities this year are going to be absolutely amazing!"

Robyn's eyes landed on Billie, who watched this performance with disdain, and Robyn's façade seemed to flicker for a moment. Then Robyn spotted Mitch and her face lit up again as she called him over to join in her interview, telling the reporter he owned the Silver Coin Hotel. Mitch brushed past Billie on his way to the reporter.

"Will all the events this weekend proceed as planned, now that the dangerous animal has been caught?" the reporter asked Mitch.

"Everything will run as scheduled, and we still have vacancies available at the Silver Coin Hotel, although they are booking up fast. But I have to tell you," he squinted toward the reporter's press badge. "Josephine. I have to tell you, Josephine, I was never really worried about that lion. The true threat to our community is the people who bring dangerous drugs into our midst. So while I'd like to invite everyone to come join us this weekend in the best patriotic festival in Colorado, if you are one of those losers who's taking Scarlet, you stay away. You have no business bringing that trash up here, and if I find out you have, you will have to answer to me, and to Mr. Briggs."

The reporter gave a nervous laugh as she pulled the microphone away.

"Will you run that?" Mitch asked.

The reporter dithered about video editing and producer decisions. Mitch pulled his wallet out of his pocket and shoved some bills at her.

"See that they run that," he said, and stalked away.

The reporter stood there in shock for a moment, then closed her fist over the bills, looking around to see who had witnessed the bribe. Billie ran to catch up with Mitch.

"What was that all about? Are you *trying* to attract a bunch of Scarlet users?"

"No," he said. "I want them to stay away so we don't have another incident while there are a bunch of strangers around."

Billie shook her head. He never seemed to understand that his reputation didn't extend very far beyond Juniper, that his threats would only be a joke to the general population of Denver. Plenty of people were likely to take it as a challenge.

He lowered his voice. "Did you figure out where we can find the monster?"

Billie hesitated. "Yeah. I think so. Why, what's your—"

Mitch waved a hand vaguely at the crowd around them. "After all this clears out, we'll go remove the real threat."

He started to walk away but Billie ran to catch him again. "Mitch, I think it's Daniel Gadbury."

"Daniel's dead."

"No, I'm pretty sure—"

He cut her off. "Daniel's already dead, okay?" he said sharply, giving her a silencing look before leaving her standing in the crowd.

"But…" Billie said helplessly, to no one.

"Okay, let's try again," the reporter was saying. "Take a deep breath."

Mouse fluttered his lips, shook his arms, cracked his neck. "Okay," he said. "Okay, I'm ready."

Billie started to walk away, trying to avoid being in the line of any of the cameras, but then she heard the reporter say to Mouse, "So you don't think this mountain lion they caught was actually the killer?" and Billie stopped, inched her way closer to hear Mouse's answer.

"No, man," he said. His hand was shaking. "But I don't… I don't think it was Bigfoot anymore, either. Something broke into my shop. Like a… it was like this demon thing. Other people in town have seen it too, I don't understand why nobody's talking about it."

The reporter thanked him for his time and made excuses to quickly move toward the other side of the crowd. Mouse trailed after, saying, "No, maybe one more take?"

Billie tapped his shoulder and he whirled toward her, wide-eyed.

"Hey," she said, holding her hands up, palms out. "I know about the demon thing, too. I've seen it. Did you say it broke into the dispensary?"

"Yeah," he said, the tension draining from his posture. "Crashed through the back door, tore some shit up. Nearly pissed myself, thought I was dead for sure."

"What did it take?"

Mouse shrugged. "I don't know, just some stuff."

"Did you have Scarlet in there?"

"Nah, man, nah, my shop is clean, fully compliant with Colorado law. Only the dankest strains of legal weed and CBD oil."

It sounded rehearsed. Billie nearly rolled her eyes. "Do you have any left?"

"Oh yeah, we're fully stocked—"

"No," Billie said. "Any Scarlet?"

His demeanor changed. "Why, you want to buy some?"

Billie cocked an eyebrow. "So you *do* have it?"

"That thing wiped me out. Went right for it. But I should be able to get some by tomorrow."

Billie chewed her lip. If she could get a hold of some to use as bait, maybe she could somehow capture Daniel before Mitch got to him. Save him, rehabilitate him instead of just 'take him out' the way Mitch intended. But tomorrow would be too late, and it would only put Mouse in danger—again—if the creature sniffed it out before Billie could figure out a way to trap him.

"No," she told him. "No, nevermind. *Don't* get anymore for now, okay?"

She'd just have to find some already in town. Did Brock have any left? With a weary sigh, she told Mouse to stay safe, and then started back toward her cabin, head down and brow furrowed in thought.

"They're saying the official story," said a voice beside her, "is that the lion had a chip and was an escaped pet, and two of the guys killed had ties to an illegal exotic animal ring."

Billie looked up to see her dad walking beside her, hooking a thumb toward the dead lion.

She lifted her hands. "I just—I can't deal with you right now." But then she stopped walking as what he'd said finally registered. "Wait, is that true?" It made a convenient story, if they could spin it: Frankie and Gil had been delivering Toby's new pet mountain lion and the animal broke free and killed them all. It was almost believable, except that Billie knew it was an utter fabrication. But did Frankie and Gil really have ties to exotic animal trade? Because if they did, then that meant Mitch had probably exploited their connections. He could have even had this lion shipped up here as a decoy. Could he manage a scheme like that so fast? "Doesn't matter," she said, and walked faster now, hoping to leave her dad behind.

And yet he continued following her, all the way back to the cabin. Caleb was still on the porch, talking on his phone to someone. She slammed the door behind her, and Caleb stayed outside. Fortunately, so did her dad. She searched for the clothes she'd left with Caleb back at Brock's house, which had her phone in the pants pocket, but couldn't find them anywhere in the cabin. She peered out the front window. There they were in the back seat of the car. And there was her dad, still standing in the front yard, talking with Caleb, who was off the phone now. Billie sighed. She waited a couple of minutes, but when he didn't go away, she pushed open the door. "Tell him to go away," she said to Caleb as she passed by on her way to the car.

She reached into the back seat and retrieved her stack of clothes.

"Billie," Caleb said as she shut the car door. "I think you should talk to him."

She stopped in her tracks. "What?"

"I've been talking to him. He says—"

"I can't believe you. You've cut off your own dad for a *lot* less than what mine did."

"Yeah, but *my dad*—" He couldn't keep the disdain out of his voice as he said the words he so rarely uttered. "—has a long, repeated history of doing shitty and abusive things and he knows damn well that he does it. Yours fucked up once. Yeah, it was a *massive* fuck-up, but…"

He faltered and Billie just stared at him, unable to believe what she was hearing.

"I just think you should talk to him," Caleb said. "At least once. He knows some things that I think you'll want to hear."

"'Sorry for killing your mom and ruining your life' isn't really going to make me feel any better."

"That's not—"

"I don't care. After all this is over, fine, I'll hear what he has to say. But right now, *your* dad is about to go track down the so-called monster and slaughter it."

Caleb looked confused. "Okay, so let him. That means you're off the hook now."

"It's Daniel."

"Who?"

"Daniel Gadbury. I'm pretty sure he was the first one to take enough to… to transform. Does Brock have any Scarlet left?"

"Huh?" Caleb asked, then shook his head. "No, definitely not."

"Do you know anywhere we might find some?"

"Why the hell would you want to?"

"To use as bait!" Billie said, exasperated. "Maybe if we catch him rather than kill him, he can be cured."

"Why?"

"*Why?* Because it's a person, not an actual monster! Because maybe I'm not okay with people just shooting someone down because they've transformed into something they don't understand. Because Juniper doesn't need yet another body on our hands. Because if Mitch just covers this up, people are going to keep taking this drug, and it's going to happen again and again." She pushed past him to the cabin's front door, not making eye contact with her dad, who still sat on the porch, watching their whole conversation.

"I know where to get some," he said suddenly, and Billie and Caleb both turned to him. "At least, I might," he said with a shrug.

"Ugh, nevermind," Billie said, and slammed the front door behind her.

The crowd on Miners Avenue cleared out, the news vans left, and someone took the mountain lion's corpse away. Billie hoped it would be disposed of, but she had a feeling it would end up taxidermied and displayed as a trophy in one of the hunter's living rooms. Billie pursued a couple of leads for Scarlet, but either everyone was out or no one was selling. Mitch's threat on the news wouldn't stop any out of towners from bringing it up here, but it would certainly stop anyone in town from admitting they had any. She realized after the first couple of calls that everyone probably assumed she was working for Mitch to sniff them out. Which, under normal circumstances, would have been a perfectly sound assumption.

These circumstances were anything but normal.

Her dad had waited a while longer on the porch, but had eventually gone away. She bounced back and forth between being glad he was gone and regretting that she hadn't taken his offer, or at least asked where he thought he could find the drug.

When Mitch called, demanding to know the monster's location, she was sitting with elbows on the kitchen table and heels of her hands pressing to her eyes.

"Just give me a minute to figure some things out." She hung up.

He called back immediately. "I want exact GPS coordinates."

"I don't have exact GPS coordinates," she said. "But he's…" She'd gone over this choice a dozen times and still wasn't sure which one was right. If she led Mitch on a wild goose chase, someone else was likely to get hurt in the meantime. Even if Daniel was caught and rehabilitated—and she still had no solid plan for how to manage that—the fact remained that he had killed four people. It's not like he'd be back home playing video games in a couple of weeks. She sighed. "He's in a cave at Shadow Ridge. About halfway up."

"That's a good kitty cat."

Billie put her head back in her hands. Caleb finally emerged from the bathroom after the longest shower she'd even known him to take. She peeked through her fingers at him. His hair was still wet, but he was dressed in flannel pajama pants and a white t-shirt, and he was rubbing some kind of cream onto his hands.

"I gave him up," she said miserably. "I told Mitch where Daniel is."

"Then it's over," he said. "You did everything you could."

She lifted her head. "You're okay with him going out there to slaughter a man? Or, at least, something that used to be a man?"

"I'm not okay with any of this," Caleb said. "But I'm less okay with a drug-crazed monster taking out my friends." He picked up his phone from the coffee table, and Billie caught a glimpse of the blisters on his hands.

"What happened to your hands?" she asked, but Caleb was frowning down at his phone and didn't answer. "Hello?" she tried after a moment.

Caleb looked up at her, startled. "Um," he said, "One of my friends from Boulder just texted me this video. You should probably see this." He sat on the couch next to her and held the phone out so they could both watch the screen.

It was a shaky smartphone video. Billie recognized the area as Pearl Street in Boulder, not because she'd ever been there, but because of the selfies Caleb used to send her when he lived down there and would go out drinking. The video finally focused on a red, winged creature as it swooped down on a crowd of spectators, snatching a young man and carrying him to the top of a bank building. The man struggled in the creature's claws. The video cut short before showing the impact as the monster's grasp faltered and the man fell from the roof.

"Guess our guy's left town," Caleb said once they'd watched the video twice. He texted *What the hell? Are you okay?* to some girl named Jennifer who had sent him the video.

Billie chewed her lip. "He didn't have wings earlier today." Nubs that looked like they might grow into wings, but definitely not the full leathery wings she'd seen in that video clip.

"Yeah, well, he didn't have the urge to murder people and eat their stomachs last week. Who knows how fast these things change."

"How could he get all the way to Boulder without being seen, though?" Billie asked. "That would take a couple of hours, at least, and he'd have to cross a bunch of major roads and highways."

Caleb shrugged. "Remember that time there was a bear in the tree outside of my dorm room? Same deal, had to come quite a ways to get that far into town, but he was just chilling up in that tree until like noon the next day before anyone noticed."

"Sure, but…" Billie trailed off.

Caleb had been tapping at his phone and now showed her a Twitter thread from the Boulder police department, the only news so far about the incident.

"An attack on a Boulder college student remains unexplained, but suspect has been neutralized," it read.

Half a dozen CU-Boulder students and other locals replied to the thread to report their version of the sighting or demand more information. A few other videos confirmed what Caleb's friend had sent, showing the creature swooping over Pearl Street, and falling to the pavement when it was shot down by police.

"So, it's over," Caleb said, swiping the app away and tossing his phone onto the coffee table.

"I'm not so sure," Billie said. She'd pulled out Caleb's laptop and was trying to map out how long it would take to get to Boulder from Juniper on foot, figure out how fast the creature might be able to fly. Something just wasn't adding up about this for her.

Still, when Mitch texted her later to say, *I thought you said Shadow Ridge?* she used some of the limited data on her flip phone to send him a link to one of the videos. Maybe it really was over, and neither she nor Mitch had to be the one to pull the proverbial trigger.

About half an hour passed before Mitch sent back, *4th tomorrow. Be there or be fired.*

# FRIDAY

Mitch and Robyn's big break in the quest to bring tourism into Juniper had come a few years back when a prominent tourism blogger had declared the Silver Coin's Fourth of July fireworks show one of the "Top Five Best Fourth of July Celebrations You Don't Know About." When Billie was a kid, some local families would get together for a barbeque along the lakeshore and set off a few big fireworks over the water after it got dark. Now, Mitch had turned the local tradition into a major production, with half an hour of sparkly explosions, preceded by a whole day of live music and barbeques and sidewalk sales and other festivities. It also usually meant a gridlock of cars both in and out of town, every driveway blocked, every bar and restaurant overflowing. And afterward, bottles floating in the lake, plastic cups rolling down Miners Avenue, miniature American flags clogging the gutters, plastic bags caught in trees and bushes. *But hey, it revitalized our small town economy*, Billie thought bitterly.

Caleb drove Billie over to the Silver Coin early in the morning, before most of the tourists started to flood in. Shop owners were setting out sidewalk displays along Miners Avenue. Robyn and her crew hung a banner across the street. A band dragged equipment into the gazebo.

"Will you come by later?" Billie asked before she stepped out of the car.

Caleb tapped his thumbs against the steering wheel, looking up at the five-story hotel. He had lived there with his dad as a teenager, but Billie knew he went back as rarely as he could. "Maybe. I don't know. I'm going to go check in with Brock."

"You never told me what happened with Tara." Though she could guess, and she didn't much like the fact that it could come back to haunt him. Not in the form a ghost, probably, but a haunting nonetheless, especially if police started to question the pet mountain lion explanation.

Caleb said nothing. Billie kissed him and then opened the car door.

Mitch put her to work hanging decorations out in the picnic area, and then, once the check-in rush started, hauling bags up to rooms. Once the afternoon barbeque kicked off, she ran the small outdoor bar along with one other bartender. The two of them could barely keep up with the crowd, and long lines formed at both of the stations.

As Billie carried yet another load of fresh glasses from the kitchen to the outdoor bar, she spotted her dad lounging on one of the plastic chairs near the buffet table. He raised a hand to wave to her. Mitch sat down next to him and leaned close to tell him something. Billie tried to pretend she hadn't seen either of them, but it was no good. Her dad joined the line, gradually inching his way up to order a gin and tonic.

Billie poured the drink, going intentionally light on the gin, and pushed it toward him, telling him the price.

"Mr. Mulligan said it would be on the house."

"Oh he did, did he?"

She looked over to Mitch, who raised his own drink toward her in a mock toast.

"Great, whatever. Take it, then."

"He's a good man. He said he might be able to offer me a job."

"He's an awful, manipulative asshole. I'm sure you'll get along great."

Billie glared at Mitch and he grinned back at her. Would he really hire her dad, forcing her to see him every day? Knowing what he had done, knowing how Billie felt about him? Yes. Yes, he would. He really would stop at nothing to make her life more miserable.

Her dad started to say something else, but she gestured impatiently to the line of people behind him, and he sheepishly stepped aside and went back toward Mitch. She kept serving drinks but her mood had really soured. As soon as she had another excuse to leave the bar, she was going to take her sweet time with it. Maybe not come back out at all.

Over the heads of the crowd, she saw Caleb and Brock arrive. Though she'd asked him this morning if he would be here, she really hadn't expected him to show up. Mitch noticed him too, and he kept a stoic expression as he watched his son scoot onto the bench of a picnic table next to some other guys from the quarry.

"Hey, Billie!" The chipper voice pulled Billie's gaze away from Mitch and Caleb. Chloe stood at the front of the line. Billie's sour mood faded a bit, replaced by a tinge of embarrassment, remembering how Chloe had witnessed her breakdown a couple of days before. But this woman had also been witness to the rocking chair, the evidence that her mother might not be entirely gone.

"Glad you stuck around," Billie told her. Though Billie often found bubbly, cheerful women obnoxious, there was something so genuine, almost childlike, about Chloe that Billie wasn't bothered by her. She was still an outsider, though. A transplant, an infiltrator. But as far as those went, Billie thought she might be alright.

Chloe waved a hand. "Oh, it's been a crazy week, but it's good for us to see that it's not always such a sleepy little town. Stuff like this isn't normal here, I know."

*Not sure it's* normal *anywhere,* Billie thought, but bit her tongue.

"So did you make an offer?"

"Oh, yes! Robyn says we should be able to close in a couple of weeks, isn't that exciting? I just can't wait."

Billie's heart sank. "The house on Shadow Ridge?"

"What?" Chloe said. "Oh, no. Aside from the… weird energy, it was a bit too small. We're going with a gorgeous three bedroom on Snowshoe Drive."

Billie tried not to breathe an audible sigh of relief. "The Watanabe's old place. Good for you."

"With the Shadow Ridge house, though," Chloe said, dropping her voice so Billie had to lean in to hear her. "Did you say you thought that was your mom?"

Billie's throat tightened. "Yeah. I never believed she'd be there, but I finally decided to look, and, well, there's *something* there."

"You know I'm a little bit psychic, right?" Chloe said.

Billie wasn't sure she believed in psychics, but with ghosts and shifters and drug-transformed demons running around, what did she know anymore? "Sure," she said.

"I think you should go back up there. Like, soon. I get the sense that she really has something important she needs to tell you."

Billie nodded grimly. "Okay. Yeah, okay. Thanks." The person behind Chloe cleared their throat, and Billie said, "Um, what can I get you?"

"Oh! Sorry, holding up the line with my chattering. I'm just so excited we'll get to be neighbors."

Billie poured the drinks Chloe asked for and slid them across the bar. "Not *exactly* neighbors."

"Everyone here will be a neighbor compared to where we're coming from. Once we're moved in," Chloe said, "we'll have to get together. Maybe have lunch or something."

"I'd like that." Billie was surprised to find that she actually meant it. They'd definitely gotten off on the wrong foot, but Chloe didn't seem so bad, and Billie was impressed that she hadn't been scared away by everything that had happened during the week.

Billie served a few more drinks, but what Chloe had said kept bugging her. The fact that her dad and Mitch were hanging out kept bugging her, too. If he really was about to hire her dad, she'd quit. That would be the final breaking point, consequences be damned. She glanced over at Caleb. Maybe she was projecting her own discomfort, but he didn't look too happy either.

Finally, she declared, "Bar's closed" to the rest of the patrons waiting in line, pointing them toward the second small bar on the other side of the party. They protested and complained, but she didn't care. She hadn't had a break in hours. She needed to pee, and she needed to get off her feet. Maybe she could even manage to eat a hamburger and talk to her boyfriend for a few minutes.

Bathroom first—there were three port-a-potties set up along the perimeter, but Billie made her way into the hotel to the tiny and poorly-maintained employee bathroom, which was only fractionally more sanitary than the ones outside. She passed by the first of the day's three ghost tours, gathering in the lobby. Mitch had hired someone from out of town to lead the weekend tours, and the guide was telling the eager ghost hunters some absurd story about the taxadermied bear.

By the time Billie went back outside, something about the mood of the crowd had changed. And she could sense, even before she saw the monster burst out of the trees, that everything was about to go to hell.

Earlier that day, Caleb had gone to check on Brock and found his friend sitting on the porch, staring numbly out into the forest in the direction of Tara's grave.

"She's really dead isn't she?"

Caleb leaned against the porch railing and said nothing.

"I thought for a while that maybe she was just lost, but if she was out there, she'd be yelling her head off. You'd be able to hear her loud ass across the whole damn mountain. And that thing that chased her... of course she's dead."

Caleb looked Brock over, confused. Had he been so wasted that he didn't remember burying the body?

"You made me bury her," Caleb said, and the words came out sharper than he'd intended. "Don't tell me you don't remember that." The secret was already a burden, and it was somehow far more terrifying to think he might have to carry it alone.

"Fuck. I don't want to, dawg. I wanted to think it was all just a bad trip or an awful dream. But it wasn't, was it?" Brock scrubbed a hand over his face. Dried blood caked across his knuckles. So he'd already been through the punching walls stage of his grief and anger. Caleb leaned forward to peek in the front door, trying to see how badly he'd trashed the place. "I can't stay in this house a second longer, dawg. Every little thing reminds me of her."

"Okay, where do you want to go?"

"I told her we were going to see the fireworks over the lake this year. I promised her."

"So, anywhere but there, then."

"No, I *promised* her. That's where we met, you know? But then we never went back after that first year. We were supposed to go this year. I meant it."

"I don't..." Caleb started to say he didn't think going to the place where he'd met his recently deceased wife would be any less painful than staying in the house they had shared, but grief wasn't logical. "Whatever you want to do, man. But what are you going to tell people?"

"Nothing, dawg."

"No, I mean, you'll have to talk to people if we go there. They're going to ask where she is. What are you going to say? That she's missing? That she left you?"

"Missing," Brock said quietly. "Yeah, like Daniel. That was the deal, right? Came home and she was just gone." He tossed a couple of pills into his mouth and swallowed them with a swig of beer. "I can do this. Let's do this."

"Okay," Caleb said dubiously.

Traffic was already gridlocked on Miners Avenue, and Caleb's car crept at five miles per hour along with the rest. Caleb pointed to the band setting up in the gazebo and the vendor tables displayed along the sidewalks and said, "Why don't we just stay here, man? Fred's has got way better food than the Silver Coin. And look, there's Jesse and Mouse." He honked, waving to the guys, and ignored the Subaru driver in front of them who stuck a middle finger out the window, assuming Caleb had been honking at them. But Brock remained set on going to the fireworks show, so Caleb pressed on through the ant trail of traffic all the way through town and around the curve to the Silver Coin Hotel. There would probably be enough people there that he could avoid his dad. Probably.

What was normally a ten-minute drive took more than an hour, and Caleb ended up parking in the ditch outside of the parking garage. Brock only complained a little bit as he hopped one-footed over to ground that was flat enough for him to use his crutches.

Caleb met his dad's gaze across the crowd almost as soon as he and Brock entered the picnic area that stretched from the back side of the hotel down to the lake. Caleb turned his head, tried to pretend he hadn't seen, and pointed to a table where a couple of their co-workers from the quarry sat.

One of the guys, Joaquin, had apparently been in the hunting party that took down the scapegoated mountain lion, and was showing off pictures of the dead feline, regaling the group with tales of how they tracked and outwitted it. Brock and Caleb glanced at each other, but said nothing.

After two beers, Caleb ventured, "What about that weird ass thing they shot down in Boulder last night?"

"I heard that was just promo for some new horror movie," Joaquin said.

"I don't think so," Caleb said. He pulled out his phone and searched, but there were no news reports, and the entire Twitter thread he'd looked at last night appeared to have been deleted. "Huh," Caleb said. Connection was slow up here, each page taking way too long to load. He still had the video Jennifer had sent him, but the conversation had moved on, so he just shut off his phone and let it go.

They played Rock, Paper, Scissors to decide who was on deck to get the next round. Caleb beat Joaquin with paper over rock.

"Damn it!" Joaquin punched him in the shoulder and headed over to the bar.

Caleb craned his neck to see if Billie was still there, and saw her closing up shop and pointing everyone to the second mobile bar on the other side of the picnic grounds. Joaquin veered toward it and beat a bunch of disgruntled people to the front of the line. Caleb waved to show Billie where he was sitting, but she disappeared inside the hotel instead.

He half-listened as Brock whined about how great Tara had been that first year when he had met her at this very event, until one of the guys said, "What happened, she leave you?" Then the conversation had Caleb's full attention, and he held his breath waiting to see what Brock would say.

"No, dawg, she—" He stopped, frowned, tried to take a sip out of an empty bottle. "Yeah. Yeah, I guess she did."

"Shit, man. She did seem pretty psycho when we dropped you off the other day."

Then Brock sat there sullen while the other guys told stories of crazy ex-girlfriends, each anecdote more ridiculous than the last.

Joaquin came back with their bottles and clanked them onto the table. Then he pulled a red vial out of his pocket and flashed it discreetly at the group. "How 'bout a little enhancement this round?"

Both Caleb and Brock reacted as though he'd just shoved a tarantula in their faces, and the other guys gave them both a weird look.

"You can't do that shit here," Caleb said. He snatched the tube away just as Joaquin unscrewed the top. A splash landed on Caleb's jeans.

"Shit, man, don't be a narc," Joaquin said.

Caleb closed his hand over the tube and leaned out of Joaquin's reach. He put the lid back on and shoved it into his pocket. He'd get rid of it as soon as they got out of here. Pour it into some kitchen grease and throw it in the trash where it belonged.

Joaquin stood up, looking ready to fight. He and Caleb were friends, but snatching his favorite drug straight out of his hands probably crossed a line. Just then, though, Mitch walked by, giving Joaquin a warning glare, and Joaquin sat back down.

"This shit cooks your nuts," Caleb said. "Makes you impotent. For real. Look it up."

They wouldn't care about it rotting their brains or making their skin peel off their bones or turning them into literal monsters. But their nuts? Yep, that should get their attention.

"You're gonna give that back to me later," Joaquin said. Caleb flipped him off.

The guys heckled him a little more, but mostly they shut up. "When are they gonna do the fireworks?" Brock asked.

"It has to be dark first, dimwit," Joaquin said.

Caleb turned toward the forest behind them. Even over the noise of the crowd it sounded like a buffalo was tromping through the trees. Then came a flash of red between the tree trunks.

"Oh, we're fucked," Caleb said a moment before the creature burst out into the clearing. It was bigger than it had been when it chased Tara, the nubs on its back extended into full-blown leathery wings, more like the creature in the Boulder video, feet and hands clawed in a distinctly demonic way. And speaking of nuts, though it seemed to be naked, its crotch was as smooth as a Ken doll. The creature's whole torso was enclosed in a thick exoskeleton.

The monster paused at the edge of the picnic grounds as people screamed and raced away from it. It sniffed the air with pointed, lizard-like nostrils. Billie had said she thought this was Daniel Gadbury, but if so, there was no glimmer of humanity left in that devilish face. The monster set its red eyes directly on Caleb, and charged forward.

"Shit." Caleb fumbled in his pocket for the tube of Scarlet, intending to throw it out toward the lake or something to deflect it away from him, but the creature was too fast.

Billie watched as the Scarlet Monster burst out of the trees with an anguished growl, flapping massive red wings that lifted him enough that his clawed feet skimmed along the ground. The crowd erupted in panic and the creature charged forward, wings tucked down now and running into the center of the picnic grounds. She gripped the railing in front of her, holding her breath. People scattered away from the creature, but he had zeroed in on his target: the table where Caleb and Brock sat. Brock stumbled away, abandoning his crutches and clambering away in a panicked scuffle. But the creature wasn't going after Brock. He was running straight toward Caleb, who watched what was coming toward him in dumb shock.

"No!" Billie yelled. She leaped over the railing and tried to run toward him, but the crowd was surging in the opposite direction, trapping her as they pressed toward the safety of the hotel.

The creature barreled into Caleb. But instead of going for the stomach like he had done with Tara, he seized Caleb in clawed feet, flapped, and took off into the sky. Billie watched helplessly as the monster carried Caleb across the lake.

Her own shouts were drowned out by the noise of the crowd. She tried to fight her way through the throng, but kept getting pushed back toward the hotel. Mitch yelled that everything was fine, no one needed to panic, but he wasn't having much success calming the scared mob. Billie got knocked down, and threw her arms over her face to deflect the stampede. Shoes kicked her forearms, tripped over her legs. Her skin started to ripple. She gulped a breath.

*Don't shift, don't shift, don't shift…*

Someone tripped hard over her, kicking her stomach and knocking the wind out of her. She rolled onto her side, curling into a fetal position, her body trying to fold in on itself and become smaller. Claws poked at her fingertips, ready to slash out and defend her.

"Don't shift, don't shift," she wheezed. No one could hear what she said over the noise of the stampede anyway.

A hand grabbed her arm and yanked her up. She stumbled, eyes blurry, skin still rippling, but followed as the hand guided her out of the crowd. Once she leaned against the railing, finally feeling like she could breathe again, her vision cleared.

Her dad held onto both of her arms now, saying, "Are you okay?"

She blinked at him. "Yeah," she said. "Yeah, I'm okay."

She turned to the lake, scanning the sky, the shore, the trees along the perimeter. No sign of Caleb or the monster.

"I have to…" She started toward the lake. But how could she track the monster if he was in the air, now? She couldn't hunt a scent trail through the sky.

"No." Her dad tightened his grip on her arm.

She looked at the hand on her arm like it was a giant mosquito she was about to smash.

"Don't try to go after it," he said.

She yanked her arms free, but he grabbed her again.

"I'll be fine," she said. "He only goes after people who have taken Scarlet."

But if that was true, then why had he gone after Caleb? Maybe she'd been wrong about why the monster was attacking. Maybe she'd been wrong about everything.

"Caleb's gone," her dad was saying while she worked all this out. "There's nothing you can do now except keep yourself out of harm's way too. He's probably already—"

"He's not dead!" she yelled, pulling her arm away again with enough force that her dad stumbled forward a step.

Mitch strode toward them now, his face hard and flushed in anger.

"I thought you said that thing was dead," he growled.

Billie threw her hands up. "A different one, apparently! The Scarlet, it can transform people. The one they killed in Boulder must have been someone else who took too much."

"That's my *son* it just flew off with!"

"And my *boyfriend*," Billie yelled back. "So what are we going to do?"

But before Mitch could yell whatever response was building up behind his flushed cheeks, Billie's phone vibrated. She pulled it out of her pocket and stared at it for a moment before what she saw made sense.

Caleb. Caleb was calling her. She flipped it open.

"Where are you? Are you okay?"

She could barely hear him. She pressed a finger to her other ear and moved away from the noise of the crowd.

"Caleb, are you there?"

"I'm here," he said in a stage whisper.

"Where?"

"I don't know. It landed near this old warehouse, like a barn? Or an old mill? I don't know. There was a garage door that was open and I managed to lure it inside, and it's trapped in here now, but... but so am I. The door we came in was propped open with a stick, but that fell and it's jammed shut now. Everything's locked, I can't figure out how to get out."

"An old mill? What are you talking about?"

Both her dad and Mitch were at her side now, demanding to know what was going on. She shushed them and covered her ear more tightly so she could still hear Caleb.

"I don't know, it's got this bright red roof, and all the windows are boarded up—shit."

A sound of scrambling, and then the call cut off.

"Caleb? Damn it." She called back, but it hung up after one ring.

"What did he say? Where is he?" Mitch demanded.

Billie related what he'd told her. "I don't know anywhere around here that looks like that. But they couldn't have gone *that* far."

"I do." Billie and Mitch both turned to look at her dad. He cleared his throat, and said again. "I know exactly where that is. Used to be a timber processing plant, but it's vacant now."

Billie patted her pockets. "Shit, he had the car keys, too."

"We'll take my truck," Mitch said.

"Can we even get out of here?" Billie asked. "The traffic…"

"I'll roll over them like a goddamn monster truck if I have to."

Billie looked back at her dad. "You can lead us there?"

He nodded. She looked him over, not sure if she believed his claim, but what other options did they have right now?

"Then let's go."

Mitch didn't have to roll over anyone else's vehicle with his oversized tires, but he did have to bump through several ditches, drive on the wrong side of the road, yell out the window at a couple of startled tourists, and make a U-turn that had Billie gripping the grab handle and scrambling to put her seatbelt on.

Fortunately, they weren't going the same direction as most of the fleeing tourists. Her dad directed Mitch to turn up the road toward the lookout, and then onto a dirt road, barely more than a path through the trees. Billie had passed right by this turnoff when she'd driven her dad up to the lookout a few days before. Mitch shifted gears and the truck crawled up the steep grade, but then the road reached a summit and started to curve downhill instead.

"Oh crap," Billie said.

"What?" her dad said.

"We're going to pass out of my territory."

"Your what?" Mitch said.

"I can't shift outside of Juniper. If we go out of my territory, I can't shift. I can't fight that thing like, like *this*."

She held up her clawless human hands, pulled a lip up over blunt, harmless teeth. It was going to be hard enough as just a mere bobcat, but without at least that advantage, how could she be any use against the monster?

"That's not how it works," her dad said.

She turned around to stare at him in the backseat for a moment before she said, "Excuse me? You don't *know* how it works. You didn't even know my mom or I could shift until you fucking *shot* her. Or did you? Did you know, and you shot her anyway?"

"I've met—there's a group of shifters down near Durango," he said. "That's what I've been trying to get the chance to tell you. Someone I was in with believed me when I told him what really happened, told me about someone he knew who could make himself look like a bear. I went to find him before I came back here, and there was a whole family of them in this house way out in the forest. It's not like you said… the shifters have some limitations, but territory isn't one of them."

Billie turned back around, leaned her head against the headrest, and blinked back tears.

"You. Don't. Know." Each word was an effort.

"If we get out of this thing alive, I'll take you down there, baby doll."

Mitch snorted at the nickname, and Billie shot him a glare, which he didn't even acknowledge.

"There." Her dad pointed, and Mitch turned down another nearly invisible road. It was overgrown, the ghosts of tire tracks barely visible beneath grass and wildflowers. The red roof of the abandoned timber mill came into view.

Mitch parked and the three of them cautiously stepped out. Billie's phone buzzed again.

"Tell me that's my rescue party out there," Caleb whispered.

"Yeah," Billie said. "It's us. Where are you and where is—" She almost said "Daniel," but opted for "the monster" instead, wincing slightly as she said it.

But before he could answer, something slammed against a second-story window, rattling the boards across the outside, and an earsplitting inhuman screech sent some nearby birds fluttering off.

Mitch pulled a gun out of his glove compartment, then opened the toolbox on the truck bed. He grabbed a crowbar and handed it to Billie's dad.

"What did you say?" Billie asked through the phone, trying to keep her voice low.

"I'm downstairs," Caleb repeated, a little louder now. "It's upstairs. For now."

There were two big industrial garage doors in the front, like the one Caleb had said had been propped open when he lured the creature in. They were both definitely shut tight now.

"Hell," Mitch said. "I'll just hitch a chain to my truck and yank the damn door off." He was already digging in his toolbox.

"Your dad's going to use his truck to pull the garage door off," Billie relayed.

"That'll let the monster out, too," Caleb pointed out.

"Crap," Billie said. She lowered the phone and caught Mitch's attention. "Let's see if we can get him out a door or window or something so the monster stays trapped inside."

Mitch slammed a tool aggressively back into the toolbox, but nodded.

"Okay, we're going to try to get just you out."

"There's a door around the back," Caleb whispered. "But it's got a big chain across it."

Billie circled around the building and found a regular door, propped slightly open, the thick chain keeping it from opening any farther.

She dropped the phone and fell to her knees next to the door. Caleb extended his fingers just barely through the gap. Billie reached for him.

"Oh my god, I thought you were dead."

"Yeah, me too," he whispered. His fingers were covered in blood.

"What happened?"

"My leg," Caleb said. He tried to pull his hand back, but Billie held tight. "Joaquin, he had a vial of Scarlet and I, like, confiscated it."

"*That's* why the monster went after you," Billie said with relief.

"Nearly clawed my leg off trying to get it from me."

"We're going to get you out of there. Do you still have the Scarlet?"

"No. I dropped it while we were in the air."

"How did you—" But before she could finish, Caleb yanked his hand back and fell away as the creature screamed again. Mitch and her dad rounded the building and found her yanking at the thick chain and heavy padlock. "Do you have anything that can cut this?"

Mitch said, "Psht," like it was no big deal, and went back to the truck, returning a moment later with a huge pair of bolt cutters. But despite his initial confidence, neither of them could get through the thick chain or the lock. Billie looked for other options while they strained. She picked up the discarded crowbar and pried at the boards over one of the windows. One fell to the ground just as Mitch yelled, "Shit!"

Billie paused and looked back over to see Mitch's bleeding hand, the bolt cutter abandoned on the ground, blood across the blade. She pried the next board loose. It would be a tight squeeze, and the breaking glass would surely attract the monster's attention, but Caleb would be able to crawl out if he were quick enough. And the monster wouldn't be able to fit, not with those big leathery wings.

The board fell to the ground and Billie wielded the crowbar straight at the glass.

It thunked and bounced back with a painful reverberation that nearly made her lose her balance. She reared back and tried again, to the same disappointing effect.

Mitch had gone back to the truck to deal with his sliced-open hand. Her dad came up beside her and she handed him the crowbar. He attacked the window once, but then said, "Storm glass. Gonna take a lot more to break it than this."

They both jumped as the Scarlet Monster slammed a red, clawed hand against the inside of the glass. The creature peered out at them with a face that had been morphed and reshaped into something no longer human. Was Daniel still in there? Could he be recovered, or had he been completely lost inside whatever this was that he had become? Or, Billie wondered, had the monster always been in there, waiting for a chance to break out?

Billie circled the building again, searching for alternate ways to get in. They might have to tear down that garage door after all. There would be no choice but to shoot at that point. And if he got away, how would they ever catch him again? Around the other side of the building was another window, this one not boarded up, and with a sign taped to the inside. Robyn's perky and infuriating portrait smiled back at her, the real estate company's logo next to it. "Call me for details about this property," the sign proclaimed, the phone number in bold below that.

"Oh no," Billie said.

The door had an electronic lockbox. Billie picked it up, pushing numbers at random, hoping she might stumble across the right code. The monster slammed against the walls and Caleb screamed.

Billie pressed one more combination, and when it blinked red, she let the lockbox fall with a heavy clunk. She found her dad and asked, "You knew where this place was. Any chance you know the combo for that real estate lock box?" He shook his head.

"Damn it." With reluctant resolve, she pulled out her phone and dialed the number on the sign.

Robyn answered with a cheery and formal greeting, the sounds of the festival in the background. Apparently the Miners Avenue festivities hadn't been affected by what happened at the Silver Coin.

"Robyn, it's Billie. I need the lockbox code to one of your buildings."

"What?" Robyn laughed incredulously. "That's not how it works. If you'd like to make an appointment—"

"The timber mill up on Firelog Drive."

"What *ever* would you want with that place?"

Caleb screamed again. Billie doubted Robyn could hear it over the background noise, wasn't sure she'd care even if she did.

"The code! Just give me the code."

Robyn hung up on her. Cursing, Billie called back again.

"I don't know what you're playing at—" Robyn started.

"This is literally a life or death situation," Billie said. "The thing that's been killing people, it's… it's here…" They needed to let Caleb out, but Robyn didn't know any of the context to understand what she was saying, probably actually believed the story of the scapegoated mountain lion. She talked over whatever Robyn was saying, deciding that she needed to take a different tactic. "Robyn, listen to me. If you give me this code, right now, I will sell my cabin. You can tear it all down and rebuild a strip mall or whatever. I just need the code. Right now. This offer expires in thirty seconds."

There was silence on the other end. Then, Robyn told her a string of numbers. Billie hiked her shoulder to hold the phone in place and asked her to repeat while she punched the combination on the lockbox's digital pad. The box opened, revealing a silver key. Billie pinched the key and lifted it reverently out.

"Thank you." She hung up while Robyn was in mid-sentence.

Billie took a shaky breath. The hair on her arms stood on end and her skin gave a slight ripple. What if her dad had been right? What if she *could* shift this far away from home, or anywhere? But she still couldn't accept it. It felt like being told *sure, you can fly.*

Then again, Daniel had.

She pushed the key into the doorknob, turned it and yanked the door open. It stuck on a mound of accumulated dirt and she had to yank again to bring it wide enough to get through.

A whimper echoed through the empty building and she struggled to pinpoint where the sound had come from. It was dark in here, the shadows broken only by a square of sunlight through the window that she'd tried to crack with the crowbar, and whatever light could sneak between the boards over the others. Some of the shadows started to coalesce into the shapes of abandoned sawmill equipment and stacks of half-rotted logs. As her eyes adjusted, she could make out a couple of rumpled blankets, a kerosene lamp, and some empty food cans. Someone had been squatting here. That accounted for the rollup door being propped open, at least.

Something scraped across the floorboards above her, and Billie looked up at the cobwebbed ceiling. Upstairs. The creature must have taken Caleb upstairs. A narrow staircase in the corner led her up there, and she braced herself for what she might see.

The second level was a little brighter. Caleb lay in a pool of blood, slumped against the wall, gripping a wooden plank. She rushed toward him.

"Caleb." She touched his cheek. "Caleb, are you with me?" His head lolled to one side and he looked up at her with a start.

"You have to get out of here," he said.

"Yes, both of us, come on."

But as she started to help him stand, her gaze fell on the creature in a corner across the room, nursing a broken wing.

The creature noticed her, too. He cocked his head and sniffed curiously, confusion passing over his unearthly face. Then he crawled onto hands and knees, injured wing dragging, readying into a crouch.

He winced as though in pain, but she had no doubt he could still take her out with one leap. Even if she could manage to shift, she didn't think a bobcat would stand much of a chance against this thing. It was going to take something bigger. Something more dangerous.

Caleb leaned against the wall and Billie stepped away from him, facing the monster. She unbuttoned her jeans.

"Billie, no," Caleb pleaded.

But it was too late. She would shift or she would die.

She had just enough time to jerk her jeans and shoes off, and the rest of her clothes stretched and broke as her body reshaped. She shook, knocking off the bits of fabric, and bared teeth at the monster.

Mountain lion teeth.

The form felt strange, like wearing shoes that were too big, or a clunky and rigid Halloween costume. She took a step forward, testing out large paws, swinging an unfamiliar tail.

The creature lunged.

Billie met him with a swift bite to the shoulder. The blood tasted the way Scarlet smelled, and she let go and spat it out, swiping claws across the creature's torso.

The Scarlet Monster pushed her away, sending her rolling across the floor. Billie righted herself and pounced again, trapping the weakened monster beneath her paws. One well-aimed bite could end this, she knew, but she wasn't sure she could bring herself to do it. Her claws dug deeper as the creature writhed beneath her. She stared at the exposed throat. If he didn't give up, she would have no choice. The sickening flavor of blood lingered on her tongue from that first awkward bite.

A gunshot split the air. Billie fell away, her human skin returning before she could control the shift. She realized she still had a scrap of shirt hanging off of one shoulder, torn during the sudden transition. Her dad stood with Mitch's gun pointed in her direction, and a scream caught in her throat as she crawled backward against the wall.

But he wasn't pointing it at her. The fired bullet hadn't hit her, though she'd felt the energy of it, the wind of its speed as it rushed by, close, *too close,* to her body.

Labored, rattling breaths raised the creature's ribcage. But he lay immobile, incapacitated. Billie's dad took another step toward him, gun still aimed. Billie scrambled toward her dad, grabbed his leg. "No, don't." He lowered the gun. Billie wiped away the tears she hadn't realized had leaked out, and found blood mingled amongst them. Whose, she wasn't sure.

Mitch clomped up the stairs then, his hand wrapped in a bloody cloth, and went straight to Caleb. Billie struggled into her jeans, uncomfortably aware of her exposed, blood-spattered breasts.

Her dad pulled off his own t-shirt and offered it to her. His ribs showed through his skin. Though his arms were strong and muscled, his skin looked like leather left out in the sun, and the few bits of hair on his chest were almost stark white. Billie hesitated, but then took the shirt, pulling it over her head. It smelled like sweat and blood, but there was something very familiar about it too, a scent signature memorable enough even her human nose could recognize. It reminded her of being pushed in a tire swing in the backyard, and being lifted off of the gravel driveway and put back onto a bicycle for the fifteenth time. She remembered squealing happily as she was thrown over his shoulder, remembered bedtime stories about the adventures of an old miner and his daughter exploring mountain caves. She wiped away more tears.

Mitch said, "Let's finish this and get the hell out of here," and her dad took a step toward the monster, raising the gun again. Billie scrambled forward.

"No, don't! That's a person under there. Despite what he looks like. Despite what he's done."

Her dad met her eyes and she forced herself not to look away. He lowered the gun, and his gaze flicked over to Mitch and Caleb. Mitch was struggling to help Caleb stand, both of them wincing.

Her dad gestured toward the Scarlet Monster—toward Daniel—still breathing raggedly on the floor, blood pooling around him. "I think he's done for anyway."

"Maybe," Billie agreed. "But none of us have to be the one who makes that final choice. He was a person, once. He still might be."

"They need to get to a hospital." He pointed toward Caleb and Mitch, both bleeding, helping each other stumble down the staircase.

"So then let's go. All of us." She pointed to Daniel to make sure they understood he was included in that.

Caleb nearly fell on the stairs, and Billie rushed to his side, swooping under his arm to hold him up, while Mitch clung to the railing. Her dad shoved the gun into his waistband and came over to help Mitch.

Downstairs, her dad left Mitch standing on his own for a moment while he went to grab a bag next to the makeshift campfire near the rollup door. He took a shirt out of it, used it to wipe off the gun, which he handed back to Mitch, then put on the shirt. After he'd slung the bag over his shoulder, he swooped under Caleb's other arm to help Billie carry him out the door and into the truck.

"We all go," Billie said when they reached the truck. "Either we wait here for the cops to show up, or we all go."

There were a lot of reasons not to wait for the cops, all their injuries not least among them. Her dad was likely to catch the brunt of their questioning, and could end up arrested again for being an ex-felon in possession of a firearm, or—Billie realized, piecing together the camp site with the fact that he knew right where to find this place—for squatting.

Her dad hesitated a moment longer, then grabbed a tarp from the back of the truck. They went back upstairs and carefully maneuvered the wheezing, probably dying, monster onto the tarp, and carried him down to the truck. Would a few ropes securing him in the truck bed be enough to keep him from breaking free? Billie doubted it, but he sure didn't look like he was going to attack anyone anytime soon.

Mitch gestured at the claw marks across Daniel's chest. "How do you plan to explain that this is what's been killing people when it looks like it's been attacked by a wild animal itself?"

"People saw it carry a man off," Billie's dad said. "I don't think they'll much care what took it down."

She shut the door to the timber mill and stuck Robyn's key back inside the lockbox.

Mitch started to climb in the driver's seat, but Billie stepped in front of him, pointing to his wrapped and blood-soaked hand. With a frustrated growl, he handed over the keys.

Traffic was heavy on the way out of town, but fortunately not gridlocked. Billie winced a bit as she passed beyond what she'd always perceived as her territory, but that belief, that limit, had already been broken. She'd shifted into a form she didn't think she could manage, in a place she didn't think would allow it.

"Do you know how to get to the hospital?" Caleb asked as she navigated the switchbacks.

She only knew that it was at least forty miles away. Forty miles outside of Juniper.

"Nope," she admitted. "That is brand new territory for me."

Billie parked in front of the Frisco emergency room and walked around to lift the tarp covering the bed of the truck. The creature that had once been Daniel Gadbury lay very still now, no wheezing breaths rattling his overlarge chest any longer, the claws of his hands and feet curled in on themselves.

"Shit," Billie breathed. They were too late. They'd lost any chance they might have had that he could be saved, brought back to his human form.

The paramedic who came out to meet them looked under the tarp and muttered, "What the hell?" Daniel was quickly transferred onto a gurney, covered up, and hurried away.

Caleb and Mitch, however, had to wait their turn for more than an hour, surrounded by people with burned faces and blown-off fingers.

"It is Fourth of July," Mitch muttered when Billie returned from giving her version of the story to the hospital's police officer. Her dad had disappeared almost as soon as they arrived, walking into Frisco and saying he'd catch up with her later. He must have known they'd be questioned, wanted to avoid it himself. Billie had left him out of her version. She wasn't quite sure how she felt about him anymore, but she knew that she didn't want him to go back to jail, especially when he'd actually done the right thing, this time.

Caleb was finally admitted. They took Mitch back a few minutes later, leaving Billie alone in the waiting room.

She stared blankly at the television on the wall. The news played silently, black subtitles at the bottom of the screen. Something about an alleged cult leader being arrested in Boulder, a number of missing college students found in bad condition. She watched the screen without really seeing it, feeling numb.

After a while, a nurse came out to find her.

"Caleb needs a blood transfusion," he told Billie. "The problem is, our blood stocks are very low right now."

"Really? How is that possible?" Billie looked around at the hospital. This was easily the largest building she could ever remember being in; the thought that they wouldn't have everything they needed in a place this big seemed absurd.

The nurse blinked at her, expression almost bemused. "Because of what happened to all of those college kids, of course."

"Oh. The cult thing?" Billie suddenly felt even smaller, almost swallowed whole by the enormity of the world. How small her territory was. Her territory. The realization that she really was well out of it made her breath quicken. Her leg bounced in agitation.

"Do you know your blood type?" the nurse asked.

"Huh? No."

"We can do a quick test and see if you might be an appropriate donor, if you're willing."

"Of course. Drain me if you need, to save him."

She let him prick her finger, and waited for the results. "The good news," the nurse said after a couple of minutes, "is your blood type is what we call the universal donor. The bad news is that we can't use it because you also tested positive for Scarlet."

"What? No, you must have mixed it up with someone else, I've never—"

"I'm not here to judge," the nurse said. "But the fact is, we can't take donations that contain that substance. We'll keep searching for another donor." He sent her back to the waiting room.

Billie rubbed the spot where her finger had bled. Had someone slipped her some of the drug without her realizing it? But she had no gaps of memory, no strange sensations this might explain. Maybe the taste of the monster's blood—Daniel's blood—had been enough to infect her? Then again, he shouldn't have attacked her in the first place if she hadn't already had it in her system. She recalled the way the... the way *Daniel* had looked at her at the mill, curious and sniffing at her like he smelled what he was after.

"Hey, kitty cat." Mitch's voice startled her out of her panicked spiral of speculation.

She closed her eyes, rested her head back against the chair.

"I really wish you wouldn't call me that."

"I know." There was no sarcasm or passive-aggressive tone to it. His hand was freshly bandaged, no longer wrapped in the greasy rag he'd initially used. A streak of dried blood stained his shirt. He crunched a cracker that he took out of a noisy plastic wrapper.

"They wouldn't let me donate blood," she told him. She didn't say why.

"They took some from me."

"Even with your injuries?"

He shrugged, suppressing a wince, and cradled his hand in his uninjured arm.

Eventually, they were allowed to go see Caleb. He was in a double room, and the person in the other bed had bandages over their entire face. Caleb looked groggy, but fairly good, considering all he'd been through.

When she leaned over the bed to kiss him, Caleb whispered, "You shifted outside of your range, didn't you?"

She grinned. "I did."

"So does this mean we can move out of Juniper now?"

Her grin faltered. She hadn't told him yet that she'd essentially traded their house for his life. Robyn would be calling to make the arrangements as soon as the Fourth of July was over, she was sure. But now she had a new tether to the town: the ghost of her mother lingering up at Shadow Ridge. Also, the timber mill hadn't been that far out of her territory—maybe her range was simply larger than she realized. To avoid having to go over all these complications right now, she asked, "Do you still want to leave?"

Caleb looked at Mitch with an expression Billie couldn't interpret.

"I did help save your ass, you know," Mitch said. "You're my *son*." The word had such a sense of possessiveness imbued in it. Caleb sighed.

Fortunately, Mitch's phone rang just then, and he answered it as he walked out into the hallway, saying, "Yeah, I know. No, tell them we're not offering any refunds."

Billie shook her head. Caleb closed his eyes. "I'll let you rest," she said. "I'm going to go find my dad and give him an update. Did they feed you yet? I hear their lime Jell-O is the best in the state." Caleb gave a tired half-smile, but didn't open his eyes. Billie kissed him on the forehead. When she passed by Mitch in the hallway, he was still yelling at one of the front desk clerks, and a nurse was trying to tell him he needed to take the call out to the waiting room.

She didn't go find her dad, though. She'd have time to talk to him later, figure out what he knew about the other shifters, what he had to say. But for now, she had a question for herself. There was a hill behind the hospital, thick with pine trees. If she could get far enough from the bike trails, she could have a few moments alone. To see if she really was still herself.

She found a spot that seemed to be out of sight from any of the trails. She removed the shirt her dad had given her, took off her jeans and shoes. She folded the clothes and laid them on a lichen-covered boulder. A chipmunk darted out of a gap in the rocks and watched her curiously. Billie stood there a moment, feeling the cool evening breeze on her skin. Then she took a deep breath, closed her eyes, and her body morphed and folded into a different form.

She opened yellow, cat-slit eyes. The chipmunk skittered back into its hole. Billie sat on her haunches and groomed her fur. Bobcat, the form she felt most at home in, even more so than her awkward human body. There would be time later to experiment with the mountain lion form again, if she wanted to. If she ever felt she really needed to. For now, this form was as familiar as a security blanket, and she needed that out in this strange new world. Her territory might have been larger than she realized, but it wouldn't extend this far. Not all the way to Frisco, dozens of miles from the peaks and ridges she called home. Caleb had been right; her dad had been right. She wasn't limited the way she had thought. Maybe she'd grown out of it. Or maybe she never had been.

Billie climbed the hill, padding across the fallen pine needles, through long shadows that striped the ground. At the top, she climbed a tree trunk and settled on a branch where she could see all around her. The hospital lay below on one side and the Dillon Reservoir sparkled in the setting sun on the other. A couple of colorful fireworks crackled in the distance. Gray and white peaks ringed the horizon.

She could climb every one of those peaks, if she wanted to. Explore new forests, cross new rivers. The world was enormous, sure, but it was also—for the first time ever—wide open for her. And if what her dad said was true, then a couple hundred miles to the south, somewhere on one of those other mountains, were more people like her.

Want to know what happens next?
Turn the page for an exclusive excerpt of *Ready, Shift, and Go*,
Book Two in the Billie Blackwater series.

Find your copy of *Ready, Shift, and Go* at Amazon,
BarnesandNoble.com, Books-a-Million, or request a copy through
your local independent bookstore.

"We're about ten miles out from Durango," Billie's dad told her. "Should be a turn coming up."

He motioned toward the maps that he'd printed out at Juniper's tiny library, which they'd used to navigate this far. She reached down and snatched up the crinkled papers from the floorboard. Her neck was stiff and her hips and lower back ached. They'd stopped only once during this long drive. She couldn't remember ever having to sit in one spot for this long before. It was awful, and she was ready for the drive to be done. She called out turns and street names that took them well off of the main roads, until they were bumping along a dirt road a lot like the one that had taken them to the old timber mill where they'd had the final showdown with Scarlet Monster. But this road went on longer than that one had, cutting switchbacks through a muddy canyon.

"Isolated," Billie commented. Of course, if they really were a family of shapeshifters, it made sense they'd want to be as far away from everyone else as they could be.

"We're almost there."

After a few more minutes, her dad made another turn onto an unmarked road, unprompted by the printed directions. A metal gate stood open, the chain coiled on the ground.

"That's strange," he said.

"They know we're coming, though, right?" Billie said. "So they'd leave it open for us."

Her dad said nothing. As he drove through the gate, she said, "You *did* tell them we were coming." But she knew he didn't have a phone, and he'd never asked to use hers or Caleb's. "Is it safe to just drive up here?"

"Yeah," Keith said, sounding like he was feigning more confidence than he felt. "What's the worst that can happen?"

"Uh, you want a list?" Billie said. Her breath was getting shorter, her heartbeat quickening.

"It'll be fine, Stan knows me."

Billie shook her head. It seemed very bad form to just show up unannounced, even if they did know him.

A two-story wooden came into view, with dark wood siding and a peaked roof. A crew cab truck was parked in front. Half a dozen chickens pecked at the ground. The door to their coop, just to the left of the house, had been left open.

Her dad parked next to the other truck and stepped out. Billie hesitated, taking a long breath before she joined him. She had so many questions to ask these people. She couldn't believe that she was finally going to meet someone else like herself. Were they really, though? And would they accept her? Billie took one more breath and then opened the door. She closed it softly behind her, and followed her dad up the steps to the wide, covered porch.

He knocked on the door, four strong, urgent taps. While they waited for an answer, Billie looked around. The wheels of the truck they'd parked next to were turned sharply, and from this side, she could see that the driver's side door was open. Shirts and overalls swayed in the wind on a clothesline in the yard, but some of the clothes had blown off and lay on the ground, and when Billie looked closer, she saw the ones still hanging had been spattered with mud. One shoe lay on its side at the edge of the porch, the other half of the pair nowhere to be seen.

Something wasn't right.

Maybe they'd heard someone driving up uninvited, and they'd all shifted and scattered into the forest? Her dad knocked again, but no one came to the door. Billie scanned the windows for any fluttering curtains, any signs someone might be peeking out. No movement at all. She turned in a circle, studying the perimeter, the forest surrounding them.

Billie pulled out her cell phone. Only one bar, but that was about all she usually had in most of Juniper, too.

"You have a number for any of them? Stan, maybe?" Stan was the main one her dad always talked about. He was supposedly a bear shifter, and the patriarch of this family.

Her dad thought for a second, and then rattled off a number. Billie punched it in.

A second after she heard the ring on her end, a ring echoed inside the house. She let it ring a few times, listening for any signs of movement inside, maybe someone waking up to go answer. Nothing. The voicemail notification told her the mailbox was full. She hung up.

Her dad turned the doorknob, and it swung open, unlocked. Billie followed, the hairs on the back of her neck rising.

"Hello?" he shouted. "Anyone home? It's Keith Blackwater. You told me come back any time, remember?"

Ants crawled over a plate of half-eaten pancakes on the kitchen table. Another plate lay in broken shards on the floor. Billie followed her dad into a living room, where some Popular Mechanics magazines had spilled off of the coffee table onto the floor. Water ran inside a small bathroom off to the side of the living room, and Billie knocked lightly on the door frame before poking her head in. It was empty, light on and the sink overflowing. She reached toward the running faucet, then thought better of it, and grabbed a towel, using that to turn it off.

*No fingerprints*, she thought. *Since I've clearly found myself in a crime scene. Again.*

There was one very distinct difference between this and Toby Moran's house, though. No bodies.

At least, not yet. Billie braced herself around each corner, each new room, expecting to stumble on a gruesome scene at any moment. There were signs of struggle, but no blood, and no corpses. She wandered back toward the living room. An odd bitter smell lingered throughout the house, something Billie couldn't identify, at least with her human senses. Her dad had climbed the stairs to the second level, and he clomped back down now, shrugging.

"I don't know what happened, but ain't nobody here. I don't like this, baby doll, not at all. We should go."

Billie started to nod, but it turned into a shake. "Wait," she said, though her throat felt tight around the word. "I can…maybe if I shift, I can figure out…something."

"What, like from smells?"

"Yeah, scent trails, residual chemicals. Things we can't see. There's something odd in the air, but I can't tell what it is."

"Okay. So…" He hooked a thumb toward the front door where they'd entered. "You, uh, want me to wait outside then?"

The thought of being trapped in this house alone made it hard to breathe. But she also wasn't going to stand here and strip and shift in front of her dad.

"Um, wait here, maybe?" She pointed back toward the bathroom. "I'll change in there."

*Change*, like she was just putting on another set of clothes.

"Sure, sure." He sat on the larger of the two couches, and Billie stepped back into the bathroom, leaving the door open a crack so she could nose it open in her bobcat form. She slid off her shoes and stood on top of them, rather than standing barefoot on this unfamiliar floor, then unbuttoned her pants, pulled off her shirt, and laid all her clothes neatly on top of the toilet seat. She stared at herself for a moment in this stranger's mirror. Then, she closed her eyes, envisioned the form, prompted the folds that would change her human body into a bobcat.

And nothing happened.

Billie peeked her eyes open, looking down at the splotches and freckles of her bare human arms. Goosebumps dimpled her arms, but her skin didn't ripple. Normally, it was easiest to shift when she felt scared. It had even happened a couple of times by accident. Most people had fight or flight instincts, but she had another option: shift. She certainly felt scared of this abandoned house and whatever had chased off the people she'd hoped to meet. So why couldn't she shift?

She closed her eyes again, concentrated, initiated the process she'd gained conscious control of when she was still a toddler. Set the creases in the paper, so to speak, that would fold her into the shape that was so natural she hardly ever had to think about it this precisely anymore. But still, nothing changed. Her human body was as rigid as a cardboard doll.

Billie reached for her clothes, started pulling them back on with shaking hands.

She'd shifted outside of what she'd thought was her territory, twice, dispelling the belief she'd always had that her powers were limited to Juniper. Her dad had assured her that these people he'd met—these people whose house she was standing in now—had told him that territory wasn't a factor the way she thought it was. What if he had been wrong? She'd come hundreds of miles, well and truly out of her territory this time. And here, she couldn't shift.

She got dressed and shoved her shoes back on. The heel was smashed down on the left one, but she didn't bother to fix it. Billie nudged the bathroom door open with her elbow and beelined for the front door.

"Did you…did you already do it?" her dad asked from the living room.

"We need to leave, now," she said.

"But I thought…"

"We need to go," she repeated, and pushed open the front door.

The chickens squawked as she hurried past them. Her dad closed the door behind them and then slid into the truck. Billie yanked at her shoe until she fixed the folded-over heel, then rubbed her hands across her arms, trying to smooth the goosebumps as the truck jounced down the driveway, away from the house.

A little ways down the road, he ran over a rock in the road, and the jolt bounced Billie practically up to the roof of the truck cab. Her skin rippled.

"Stop the truck," she said.

"Huh?"

"Stop the truck!"

Her dad brought the truck to a stop in the middle of the road, since there was no shoulder to pull over to, and no competing traffic. Billie opened the door. She headed down toward the stream that ran along one side of the road, stripping her clothes off as she went, and by the time she reached the water, she was a bobcat. Shifting always gave her a sense of freedom, a relief from all of the burdens of the human world, and she'd never felt that so keenly as she did now, peering down at the water, seeing her own cat face look back at her from the rippling reflection. She ran a few paces, turned in a circle, chasing her own bobtail. Territory *wasn't* an issue, then. But *why* could she shift here, and not back at the house?

Back in human form, she collected her clothes and got dressed as quickly as she could. Her dad was leaning against the truck, conspicuously turned the other way, as though she'd gone out into the forest to pee.

"I couldn't shift back at the house," she explained.

"Nerves?" he asked.

She shook her head. "I'm not sure. Sometimes..." She remembered almost losing her bobcat form in front of the hunters who had treed her back in Juniper. "I guess sometimes my instincts decide I'm safer in human form."

He frowned and got back into the truck. Billie followed.

"I suppose we'll go into town now," he said. "See if anyone can tell us what happened."

# ABOUT THE AUTHOR

**Kira Brinamon** grew up in the Rocky Mountains and now lives near the Rio Grande. She holds degrees in Creative Writing from the University of New Mexico and the University of Colorado, Boulder. When not writing, you can often find her at a yoga studio or on a hiking trail. Find her on Twitter @KiraBrinamon or at www.KiraBrinamon.com

# ACKNOWLEDGEMENTS

Lots of people helped shape this book into what it became, though all weaknesses and failures of its final form rest solely with me. Thank you to everyone at the 2015 CSSF Novel Workshop for helping me totally restructure after I'd written myself into a corner, especially Kij Johnson, Barbara J. Webb, and Tod McCoy. Thanks to Trysh Thompson for an emergency beta read that turned out not to be as urgent as I thought, but was still extraordinarily helpful. Thanks to the members of Critical Mass for feedback on this and so many other projects. Extra special thanks go to Emily Mah for her help on practically every stage of this book's existence. And finally, thank you to all of the other authors involved in the *Midnight Whispers* box set, where this book first found an audience.

Thank you for reading!

Please leave an honest review at Amazon, Goodreads, or wherever you discuss books online.

Leaving a review shows support for the author and helps readers like you find new books they'll love.

Please sign up for Kira's newsletter for news about upcoming titles, giveaways, special discounts, & more.

KiraBrinamon.com/newsletter.html